THE BIG GAME

EMILY SILVER

TRAVELIN' HOOSIER BOOKS

Copyright © 2022 by Emily Silver

All rights reserved.

This is a work of fiction. Names, characters, places and incidents are either the product of the author's imagination or are use fictitiously. Any resemblance to actual persons, living or dead, businesses, companies, events or locations is entirely coincidental.

No part of this book may be reproduced in any form or by any electronic or mechanical means, including information storage and retrieval systems, without written permission from the author, except for the use of brief quotations in a book review. For more information, please email the author at authoremilysilver@gmail.com.

Cover Design by Kari March Designs

Editing by Happily Editing Anns

www.authoremilysilver.com

❦ Created with Vellum

To the Indianapolis Colts…thanks for all the memories. Good, bad and everything in between.

May 2023 be BOTH of our years!

#ForTheShoe

Chapter One

JACKSON

"You're not doing it right!" comes a whiny voice.

"How am I supposed to do it?"

"It's green then blue," Noah chides. "It looks cooler for my space station."

I smile. "Sorry, bud."

He scoots over on the floor, plopping into my lap. "It's okay, Daddy. You don't know everything."

I bark out a laugh. "I'm glad I have you to teach me." I drop a kiss in his hair.

"Do you really have to leave tonight?"

Break my fucking heart, kid.

"I do. But everyone is going to be here, so you won't miss me."

"Will Grandma and Grandpa bring me a new toy?"

I smile. "I'm sure they will."

"Maybe new building bricks." He goes back to working on the project in front of him.

"Remember what we talked about, buddy?"

Noah nods at me. "Be good for Mommy."

"That's right. And in just a few days, Daddy will be home and we can play whatever games you want."

His tiny lip sticks out. "I'm going to miss you."

I scoop him up into my arms. He smells like crayons and dirt from playing outside. "I'll miss you even more."

Shuffling from down the hall has me standing. Tenley waddles into the kitchen, looking more uncomfortable than ever. The moment she sees Noah and me, her eyes start glistening.

"Go play for a minute, bud. I need to talk to Mom."

He smacks a kiss on my cheek before running back over to his pile of building bricks.

"How was the doctor's appointment?"

Tenley wipes a tear from her eye. "Baby girl is snug as a bug in there. Looks like she won't be coming anytime soon."

I breathe a sigh of relief. "Thank God." I already hated that I had to miss Tenley's appointment today because of a sick babysitter and no grandparents, but a rowdy preschooler would not sit still if we went with her. "So no chance the baby is coming this weekend?"

Tenley shakes her head. "No. The only thing you have to worry about is winning the game."

I immediately knock on the closest surface. "Don't jinx it!"

"That's bad luck, Mommy!" Noah chimes in from the living room.

"See?" I nod my head in his direction. "Even a five-year-old knows you don't say that!"

Tenley rests her crossed arms on top of her baby belly. We got lucky the first time with Noah. It took a lot longer and a lot of help to get this baby to come along. I'm fucking ecstatic it's a girl.

"Fine. Then just go and practice and play well. Happy?"

I see the smile she's fighting. I rub my hands over her belly. "I'm going to be even happier when we get to meet this little one."

Warm hands rest on top of mine. "I can't wait for her to be here."

"Just a few more weeks." I press a soft kiss to her lips. "When does everyone get in?"

Tenley brushes past me, sitting down on the oversized sofa in the living room. I feel better knowing that Tenley and Noah won't be alone while I am gone. "Your parents will be here tomorrow. Penny's flight gets in"—she stops to think—"I don't know. With the time change in Vietnam, I really don't know. And my parents will be back from their trip on Thursday."

"I'm glad the doctor said everything was okay. I hate not being here." I drop down next to her, pulling her into my side.

"We'll be okay, won't we, Noah?"

The kid in question runs up and jumps into my lap. "Mommy said we could have a special night and I can watch whatever movie I want and read three books before bed!" He holds up three tiny fingers.

"You have the best mom, kid."

"The bestest!" He wiggles out of my arms and goes back to playing with his tiny bricks. Kid's obsessed.

"I agree." I squeeze Tenley closer to me.

"Will that be what my Mother's Day mug says this year?"

"I can think of a few other things to add that you're the best at," I whisper in her ear.

"Ugh. Don't tease me with all the things you want to do to me when I can't do a thing."

"Until then, whatever you need, I'm at your beck and call."

Tenley's hand clasps my neck, pulling me closer to her. "I don't know what I'd do without you."

"Believe me, I never want to think about that." I take her lips in a deep kiss.

"Eww. Stop kissing," Noah whines.

And to think, all those years ago, if Coach hadn't helped pull my head out of my ass, I'd be missing out on all of this.

Grossed-out kid and all.

We're one game away from winning it all. From being at the top of the NFL. It's so close, I can fucking taste it. I want nothing more than to bring home that trophy.

But I know if we don't, I'll be okay. Because of the woman beside me. And the little kid who stole my heart when he came screaming into the world all those years ago. And the new little one that will be here soon.

Because these people are what matter most.

Not some trophy.

Except…

I really want to bring that thing home.

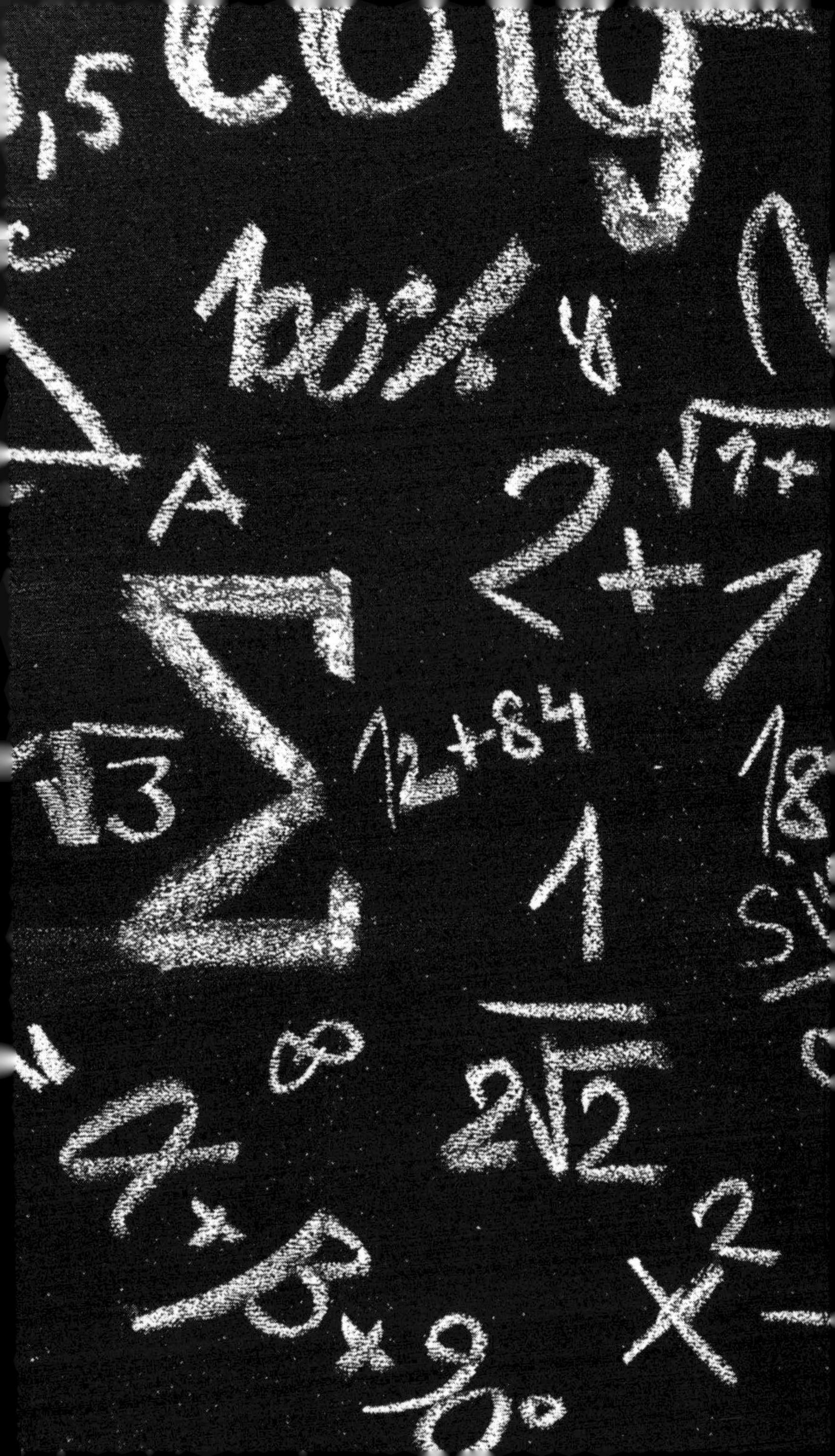

Chapter Two
CARTER

"Angie! We have to leave for school. Are you almost ready?"

"Coming, Papa!" the tiny voice yells from upstairs. "Can we call Daddy one more time?"

The sound of stomping boots pulls my attention away from the news on the TV. As much as I shouldn't be watching coverage of the Mountain Lions, I can't help it. Every single statistic is running through my brain—good and bad—on how this can go for the team.

"Daddy has practice this morning, so we might not be able to," I say, gulping down the last dregs of coffee.

"But I have to show him my outfit!"

Angie comes around the corner in a blur of color. Rainbow leggings, pink tutu, and a number eighteen Mountain Lions jersey. It's school spirit day, so she got to pick out her outfit.

I don't try to fight the smile. This girl has always marched to her own beat. "We have to be fast, okay?" I hand her my phone.

"Yes." She makes fast work, pulling up Alex's number

as I stand next to her, waiting for the FaceTime call to connect.

"Hey. Who's calling me so early?" Alex's tired voice fills the screen before we see his face.

"It's us, Daddy!" Angie is brimming with excitement.

"My two favorite people." Alex's smile is wide as he stares back at us. "Shouldn't you be at school?"

"I had to show you my outfit." Angie pops up, turning to show herself off. "Do you like it?"

"I love it. Very colorful."

"Our teacher said it was spirit day. We can wear whatever we want, but we have to support the Mountain Lions."

"Smart teacher."

"She's very smart, Daddy. Will I get to see you before the game?"

Alex shakes his head. "After the game. You and I will get to have our very own special day together and do whatever you want. How does that sound?"

"Can we get ice cream?"

"Anything you want."

"Yay! Papa, did you hear that?"

I nod. "I did. We have to leave for school. Go put on your coat and let me talk to Daddy real fast."

"I love you! Win big!" Angie blows a kiss and is off.

"I love you too." Alex lies back down. "I hate to think how disappointed she'll be if we lose."

"Don't even say it. You'll get over it. Angie? Not so much."

Alex laughs, moving the camera closer to him. "I miss you guys."

"I know. Only a few more days and then you'll be home. You feeling good?"

"Yes. I've run through the first drive so many times, I

can do it in my sleep. Hopefully we'll have the crowd on our side."

It's one of the rare times a Super Bowl is being played at the home team's stadium. Tickets are going for over five thousand dollars. I don't know who can spend that much on tickets, so it's anyone's bet on what the crowd will look like.

"You'll have us cheering for you."

"I'm sure I'll be able to hear you from the sidelines."

I point a finger at him. "Don't doubt us. That girl has a set of lungs on her."

A beep from Alex's phone has him frowning. "I need to get down for the players' meetings. I'll see you Sunday?"

I nod. "I know you won't need it, but good luck."

Alex opens his mouth to say something, but closes it. Nerves seem to be taking over as he voices the worst scenario happening. "What happens if we don't win?"

"Then you'll come home to Angie and me. We'll take a vacation like we did last time and everything will be okay."

That has Alex smiling. "And if we do win?"

I return the smile. "Then you'll come home to Angie and me. We'll take a vacation and celebrate."

"That sounds pretty damn good to me."

"I know. Now go play the game of your life. I love you."

"I love you." Alex ends the call, and I blow out a nervous breath.

At this point, I don't know who's the most nervous. But I don't have time to think as a number lights up my phone that I didn't think I'd be seeing for a while.

"Chelsea, hi. This is a surprise."

Angie comes running back into the living room, her coat haphazardly buttoned with her backpack that could swallow her whole hanging from her back. "Ready, Papa!"

Grabbing my keys, I walk out the door with her.

"Sorry to call this week, but I figured you'd want to know."

I gulp down a breath of cold mountain air as I open the car door for Angie. "Is everything okay?"

"It was a false negative."

"What?" I nearly drop the phone at our surrogate's words.

"I don't know what happened, but I still wasn't feeling well this week, so I went to the doctor. They confirmed it. I'm pregnant."

"Holy shit!"

"Papa…" Angie's words come from the back seat.

"Sorry, sweetheart," I whisper to her, covering the phone. I buckle her in and shut the door. "You're serious, Chelsea?"

"I can send you everything I got at the doctor, but looks like that baby will be coming a lot sooner than you thought."

"This is incredible. How are you feeling?" I'm awestruck.

"Morning sickness mostly, but other than that, good. Do you guys want to meet for dinner next week?"

On top of everything going on this weekend, the best news we could have possibly gotten comes today. "Yes. Let's plan something."

We talk a bit longer before hanging up the phone. Tears gather in my eyes as I get in the car.

"Are you okay, Papa?"

"Better than okay."

Because no matter what happens this weekend, our lives just got infinitely better. A win would make it that much sweeter.

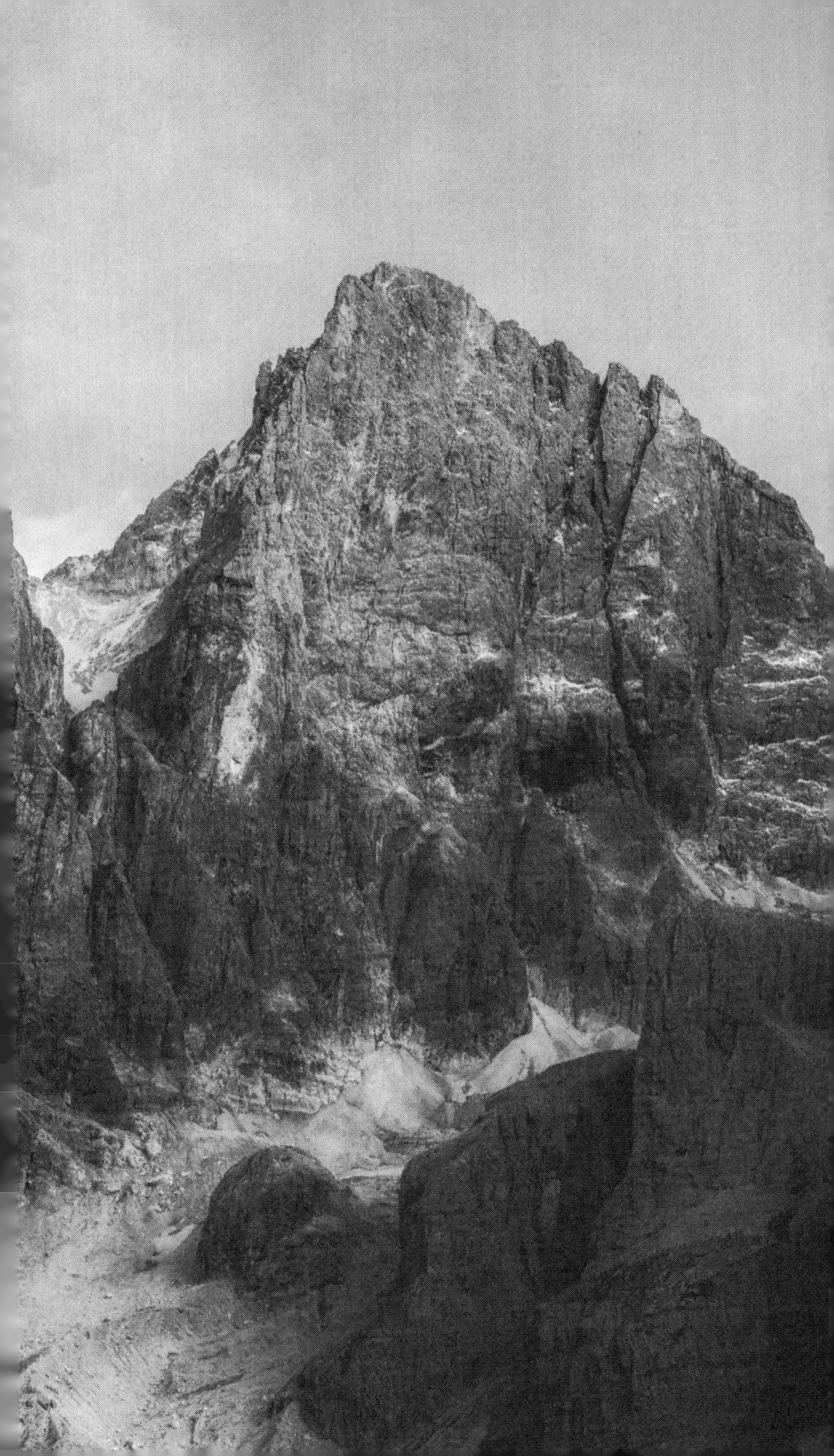

Chapter Three

PEYTON

"Colin. Pay attention to the defense. Look at the way this guy pulls up when he thinks he's got the receiver beat. Cut to the right to beat him."

"Rocky. We've watched this fifteen times. There is such a thing as overpreparation," Colin mutters into my shoulder.

We've been staying at the team hotel all week. Even though the game is being played in Denver, we've been here since Tuesday.

Every team stays together during the Super Bowl. With practice and media days, it's easier to shut the noise out when you're all together.

And that means sneaking into Colin's room when I can.

"I'm sorry. We're in the Super Bowl. I'm freaking out."

The big game is tomorrow. Curfew is in an hour, and I'll be out of here well before then. Because I'm not doing anything to jeopardize this team's chances of winning.

Every single one of these guys has fought hard to get here. To be in this position.

I couldn't be more proud of them. Having been promoted to Communications Director last year, I know everyone here.

And I've come to love them like my second family. I want this just as bad as every man on this team.

"Do I need to loosen you up?" Wrapping an arm around my waist, Colin throws me back against the bed. There's a heat in his eyes that has warmth gathering between my legs.

"Is this a good idea?" I wrap a hand around his neck, pulling him down. "It won't be too much of a distraction?"

"Rocky." Colin dips down, kissing my exposed shoulder. "It would be more of a distraction if I didn't have this. You'd be doing a disservice to Denver fans everywhere by not having sex with me."

I bark out a laugh. "Is that how you want to play this?"

He nibbles on my collarbone. "If it means you have sex with me to shut my brain up about the Super Bowl tomorrow? Then yes."

Pulling his head up to mine, I lock eyes with him. "That's all you had to say. When have I denied you anything?"

"I fucking love you, Rocky."

We shed our clothes, the only light in the room casting Colin's hard body in a warm glow. We kiss and touch each other like only we know how.

Every touch, every whispered word of love is felt as he slips inside me. Every thrust of his hips has my need growing higher and higher, eventually spilling over and taking him with me.

We're tangled up in bed, basking in the love we have for each other.

"I'm nervous about tomorrow."

The Big Game

I rest my hand over the beat of Colin's heart. "I know. It's okay."

"You're not going to try and talk me out of it?"

Colin shifts, lying on the pillow to face me.

"No." I drag a finger down his cheek. "You'll be nervous whether I tell you you'll be great or not. But I do have something that might take your mind off it."

"If it's more sex, sign me up." A cocky grin spreads across his face.

"Funny." I reach across him, grabbing my phone from the nightstand. Clicking open the photos app, I pull up the video I took earlier this week.

"What is this?"

I roll my eyes. "Hit play."

Colin does, and Waffles's face, along with our new black lab, a girl named Pancake, fills the screen.

"Waffles and Pancake!" A smile lights up Colin's face. "Hi guys!"

I can only smile at him. He loves these two so much. Maybe more than me some days.

It's debatable.

"Alright, guys. Who's going to the Super Bowl?" I ask them in the video.

Waffles cocks his head and Pancake lies down. Neither of them understand a word I'm saying.

"Can you spin and show me what you're wearing?" Holding a treat in my hand, I get them both to spin and show off their new jerseys. Waffles has always had his own 'James' jersey. But now, each of them are proudly donning number eighty-seven.

"Damn. They look good. Reppin' Dad like that." Colin flicks his gaze up to meet mine.

"There's more." I point his attention back to the screen.

"Okay. Can you both wish Daddy good luck?"

Waffles barks and Pancake comes toward me, licking the screen.

"No, Pancake. What have I said about licking the screen?" It shifts around so it's me with Pancake in my lap and Waffles at my side. Waffles, now over seventy pounds, gets in on the action, licking my face too. "We love you, Colin. Win or lose, we're always your biggest fans."

Colin tugs me into his lap, holding me in his arms. "I love you so damn much. I don't know what I did to deserve you."

I kiss every part of him I can find. "You mean everything to me, and this life wouldn't be nearly as wonderful without you in it."

Colin's phone chirps, signaling curfew is getting close.

"I wish you could stay here all night."

I hop off his lap, getting dressed. "I know. But I'll be seeing you soon enough."

Putting on his boxers, Colin walks me to the door.

"So what do you think—one hundred yards and two touchdowns tomorrow?"

"Colin! Knock on wood!" I knock on the door.

"We do this every game. If we don't do it now, it'll be bad luck. So whaddya say? Think I can do it?"

We've always done this. Colin saying what he wants to happen in the game. If it happens, we celebrate. If not, I review game film with him to see what went wrong. Usually it doesn't help, and we end up having sex, but it's our tradition anyway.

One I can't break now.

"One hundred yards and two touchdowns. Make sure to impress me."

"So full of sass," Colin says, pulling me back in for a toe-curling kiss.

The Big Game

"I love you."
"Love you, Colin."

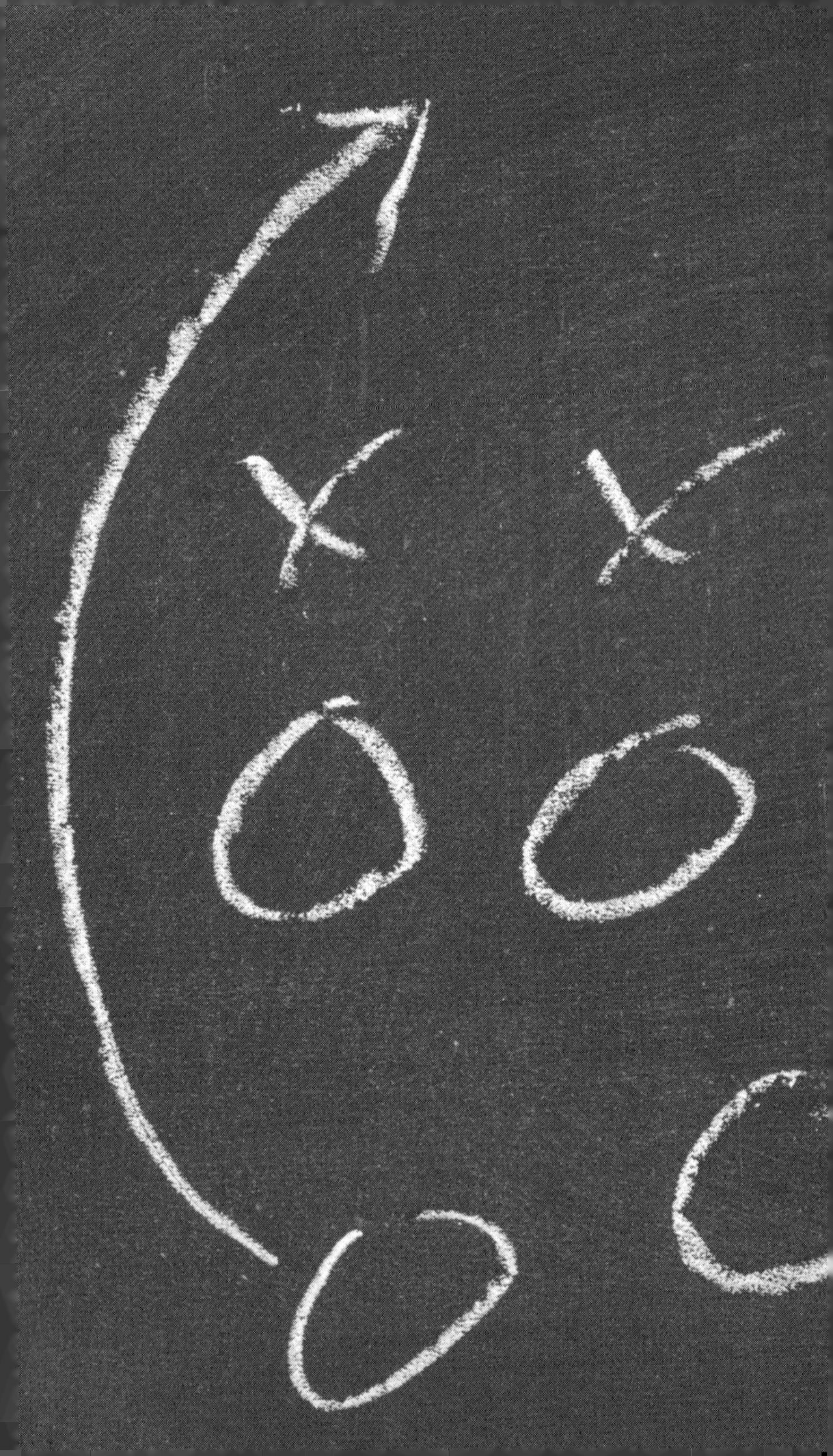

Chapter Four

FRANKIE

My vision blurs as I review the offense one more time. Watching how the receiver cuts toward the sideline, I make another note on how we can account for this during the game.

It's the same as yesterday.

And the day before.

But tomorrow is the Super Bowl. The biggest game of all of our lives.

And I'm not leaving a thing up to chance.

A knock at the door pulls my attention away from my replay of LA's conference championship game. Peering through the peephole, Knox's cocky face grins back at me.

"What are you doing down here?" I ask, swinging the door open to him.

"You didn't think I'd *not* see you the night before the Super Bowl, right?"

"You're incorrigible." Knox brushes past me into the room, his scent lingering in the small space.

"We've been doing this for how many years now?" Knox drops down onto the bed, leaning against the headboard. In nothing but gray sweats and a tight Mountain Lions shirt, he's every bit as sexy as he was the first day I met him.

"Just a few." I flop down on the bed next to him, pulling his oversized tee that I sleep in around my knees. "How are you feeling about the game tomorrow?"

"I should be asking you the same thing," he deflects.

"I'm nervous. I know everyone is ready, but I keep thinking about what happens if we screw up the game plan. It's the Super Bowl. Who knows what will happen when the guys get out on the field? A million and one different things could happen and—"

Knox leans forward, taking my lips in a heated kiss, shutting off my train of thought. I groan as his tongue slips inside my mouth. Knox is unhurried as his hands move up my thighs, and he pulls me onto his lap

"I'd say we shouldn't be doing this, but it proves to be a pretty great stress reliever." Knox's voice is gravelly as he kisses his way down my neck.

I rock over him, feeling him harden beneath me. "Very good indeed."

The noise of the TV intrudes in the quiet room.

"Why are you watching the game again?" Knox grabs the remote on the nightstand and turns it off.

"Trying to glean any last-minute plays if I can. LA is a good team."

"We're better." Knox tucks a lock of hair behind my ear.

"I know. I just"—I blow out a breath—"I want this more than anything. For me. For you. For this team. I still feel like I have to prove myself."

"You don't have to prove a damn thing to anyone. You're the best coach out there, Frankie."

The Big Game

I play with the gold chain hanging down Knox's chest. The one his grandpa gave him all those years ago.

"It feels like I need to win this game so I don't have to keep proving myself to everyone."

I've been coaching in this league for over a decade, and I hate that I still feel this way sometimes. An announcer cracks a joke every now and then, and it feels like I'm fighting to show the men in the world that I can do this.

Knox takes my face between his hands, his thumbs brushing over my lips. "We'll win it. And when we get that trophy, that will shut up every naysayer out there."

"I love you."

"I love you." Knox shifts, bringing me closer to him. "Do you remember what we talked about all those years ago?"

Heat floods my face as I remember that talk after his grandma's funeral. It's been in the back of my mind all week.

"You're not doing it now, are you? I said we had to win one."

He smiles. That same dimpled grin that sends sparks shooting through me. Even after all these years, one look from him and I'm a puddle. "It's Super Bowl weekend. So tonight or tomorrow. Which do you prefer?"

"You can't propose to me before the Super Bowl!" I shriek, smacking him on the chest.

"It's not like you didn't have proper notice. We've been talking about this for years."

"What if the worst happens tomorrow and this weekend will forever remind us of it?"

Knox laughs at me. "If that happens, don't you think you'll want a happy memory from the weekend?"

"Why are you stressing me out with this right now?"

"Bet you haven't thought about the game in at least two minutes."

I roll my eyes as Knox leans in for another kiss. "Okay, yes, but that doesn't mean I'm not thinking now that you're going to propose and jinx us!"

"You're as bad as any player, Frankie."

Knox shifts around on the bed, reaching for something in his pocket.

"I swear, if you pull out that ring, I'm going to say no."

Knox smirks as he pulls out his phone.

"God, I hate you, you know that?"

The devil himself would fall at his feet at the smile he gives me. "You love me."

I roll my eyes at him. "Why, I don't know."

"I can think of many reasons…" His voice trails off as he peppers my neck with kisses.

"As long as those reasons are kept to yourself until tomorrow night."

"Fine." Knox spins around, pressing me back on the bed. His face hovers inches from mine. "But make no mistake, Francesca Rose. There will be more than one ring given out tomorrow night. Consider this your notice."

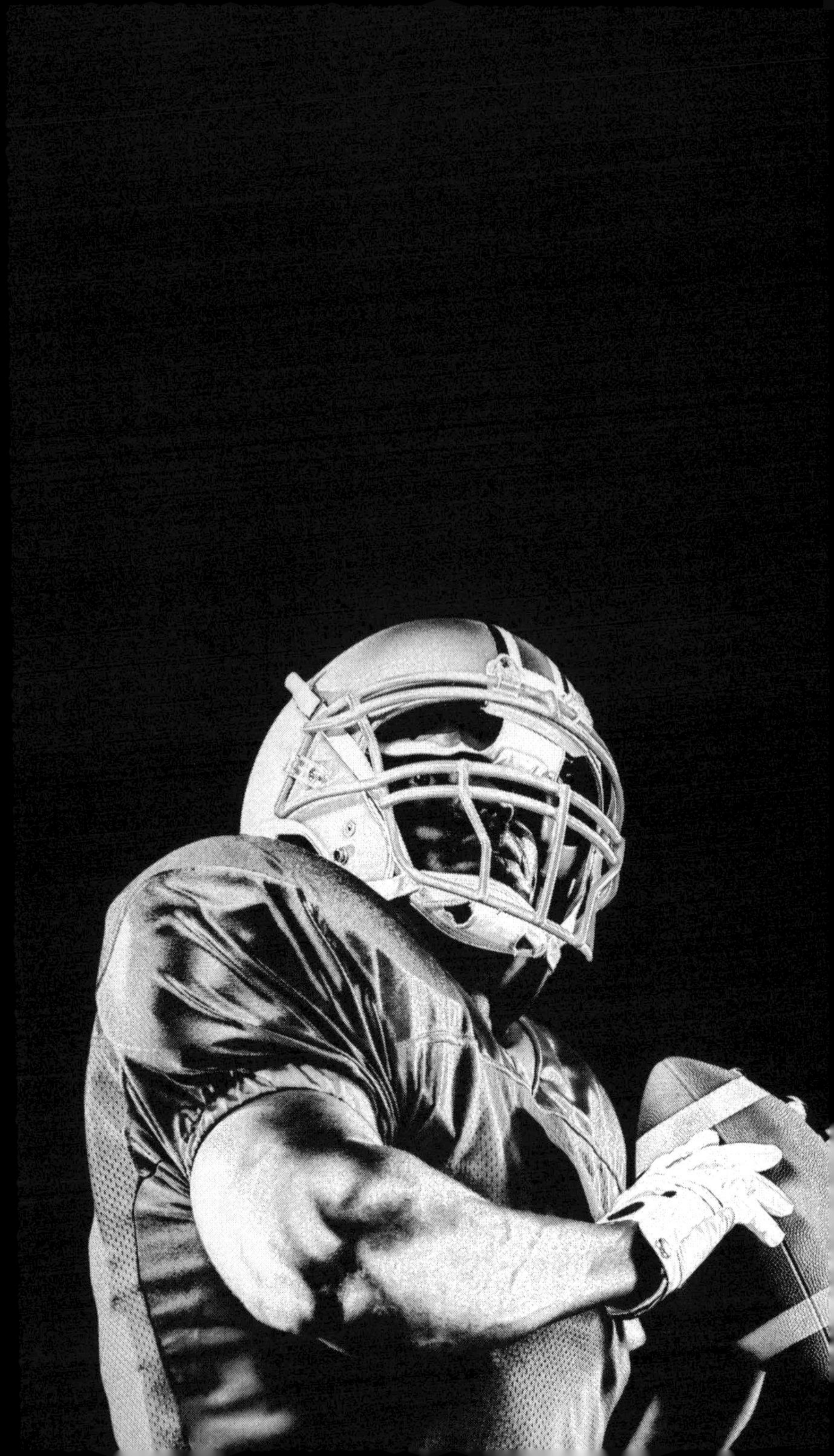

Chapter Five
ALEX

"Is there a reason we're all breaking curfew tonight?" Knox claps me on the back as the guys funnel into my room.

"Who would've thought? Knox Fisher not wanting to break the rules," Logan laughs.

Knox flips him off. "Curfew is in thirty minutes, asshole."

"So we're not breaking any rules then."

I feel like a proud dad, watching these men come together. "Don't worry, it won't take long."

"We're playing in the Super Bowl tomorrow," Logan says, awe filling his voice.

"I don't think I'll be able to sleep tonight," Colin says.

"How about a nightcap?" I pull out the lone bottle of bourbon that was in the minibar.

"I don't think that would affect a baby," Knox jokes.

"Then it won't hurt us to have a quick drink before tomorrow. I don't know about you guys, but I need to settle my nerves."

It's been on and off all day—the nerves and the

anxiety of playing in the big game tomorrow. Every kid who played backyard football wanted to lift that trophy. It's everything we've worked toward in our professional careers and it's finally here. I was fine yesterday when I got off the phone with Carter and Angie, but after running through our game plan again today, it finally felt real.

It's here. After spending a decade giving everything I have to this game, it's here.

It's not just another game.

It's the Big Game.

The fucking Super Bowl.

Pouring a splash in each glass, I hand everyone their drink.

"How you doing, Jackson?" He's staring out the window, facing the Rockies.

"Ya know, I've dreamed about this since I started playing football. And the only thing I can think about is Tenley."

"How's she doing?" Knox asks, sipping his drink.

"Doctor said she's good. Doesn't mean I'm not worried."

"What if the baby comes during the game?" Logan asks. "You should name her Lombardi."

Jackson smacks him on the back of the head. "Don't even joke about that. I can't miss my daughter's birth."

"Logan is joking." I pierce him with a hard stare. "Don't get him any more worked up."

"Besides, Lombardi would be a terrible name for a girl," Colin states.

"Hey, maybe it'll take his mind off the game," Logan says.

"Don't worry. I'll be focused during the game. Just worry about running the damn ball, Logan," Jackson retorts.

The Big Game

"And you just worry about making those field goals."

"I think we all know how to do our jobs at this point. It got us here, right?" I look over at Colin. "Ready to catch some balls?"

"There's a bad joke in there somewhere," Logan says. "I'm going to do the mature thing and bypass it."

"Holy shit. It only took playing in the Super Bowl to get the kid to grow up." Knox ruffles his hair as Logan tries to push him off.

"Are we going to get a toast, Alex?" Colin elbows me in the side. "That's why you called us, yes?"

I laugh, staring into my own drink. "Am I that obvious?"

Colin holds up his thumb and finger an inch apart. "Maybe a little."

"It's the biggest game we've ever played in. I couldn't just let the moment pass us by."

"Alright, let's hear it." Knox leans against the dresser. There's an easy smile on his face.

"You are way too calm for me right now." Colin waves a hand in his direction.

"You would be too—"

"No one wants to hear about your sex life, Knox," Jackson cuts him off.

He smirks. "If that's what you think, sure, let's go with that."

"Changing the subject," Logan cuts off any further comment between these guys. He nods to me, giving me the floor.

"I don't think I need to tell you guys how big the game is tomorrow." I look at each man standing in front of me.

"Just another Sunday, right?" Colin smiles at me.

I smile back. "There's going to be a lot of pomp and circumstance around the game, but yeah, just another

Sunday. We've gone over our game plan. If we stick to it, we'll be good. LA is a tough team, but we've battled to get here. It's been a tough few years. We should've been here before now, but it doesn't matter. We're here now."

"Fucking Vegas," Knox mutters.

It's the loss that stings the most—losing to our archrivals. We all still feel it, even after all these years.

"We can't think about that. Not now. It's finally our time." I raise my glass and everyone follows suit. "There is no one I would rather be in this game with than you. Than this team."

I look at every man here. From the time we were all drafted, our lives have changed for the better. Husbands. Wives. Kids. Dogs. Family.

"Each and every one of you is like a brother to me. And no matter what happens tomorrow, we'll still be a family…still be a team. Win as one, lose as one. No matter what happens. To the Mountain Lions!"

"To the Mountain Lions!"

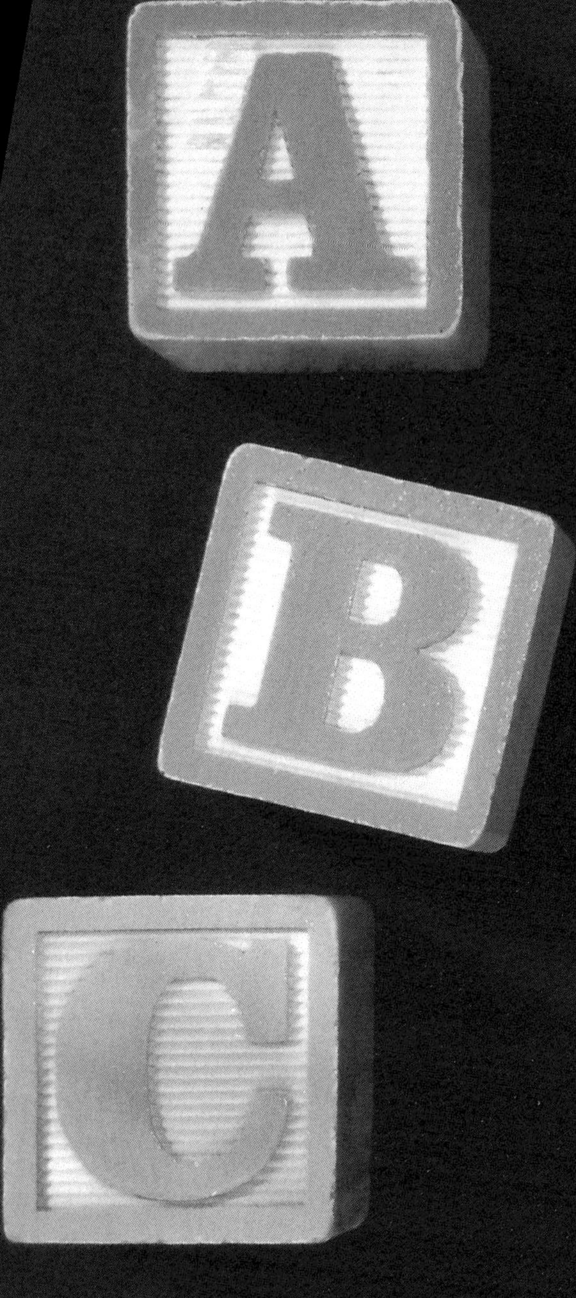

Chapter Six

TENLEY

"Aunt Peyton, can I get more nachos?" Noah asks, cheese smeared across his face.

"I don't know. Is it okay with your mom?" she asks, getting down on his level.

"Mommy, can I have more nachos?"

I smile, rubbing my belly. "Sure. Just don't eat too much."

"Yes!" He pumps his little arms up. "Maybe I can have an extra cookie too!"

"Noah…"

"What?" He shrugs his shoulders and follows Peyton inside the suite.

I turn my focus back to the game. After Alex threw a pick-six early in the second quarter, you could see shoulders sag. The Mountain Lions faithful don't trust that they can come back. But Alex is driving them down the field.

After a few minutes, Peyton sits down next to me.

"Do they know they're not making this easy on us?" I rub my belly, staring at the scoreboard. Denver is down 21-3 as Jackson runs out to hopefully close the gap.

"Deep breaths, mama. Still plenty of football to play," Peyton says, squeezing my shoulders.

"Is Noah still eating?" I peer around her, trying to see where he is.

"He's with your mom. He wanted to show her his new jersey."

I smile. Jackson gave him a new one with a Super Bowl patch before he left. He couldn't have been more excited.

"Thank God they're here."

As Jackson's kick sails through the uprights, a twinge settles low in my back. One that I've been ignoring all day because Braxton-Hicks contractions have been plaguing me for the last few days.

"Are you okay?" Peyton asks. "Your doctor said it was okay that you came, right?"

Baby girl Fields is due in three weeks, but I'm praying she makes it at least a few more hours.

"It's fine. I just can't get comfortable." I shift in the chair, trying to find a better spot. "I feel like a whale."

"You look beautiful. Motherhood suits you." Peyton gives me a bright smile. She's become a good friend these last few years.

My smile matches hers. Not long after we got married, Noah appeared in our lives. He's our pride and joy, and there's no one he loves more in the world than his dad.

"Mommy, did you see Daddy's kick? He made it!" He throws his little arms into the air before jumping into the seat next to me.

"I did. A few more of those and Denver will be right back in it." I say it more to myself, stressed at how far behind Denver is.

"Daddy will do it!" Noah wraps his arms around my belly as we both focus on the last two minutes of the half.

"Sissy. You're missing all the fun. Daddy is in the Super

The Big Game

Bowl and I really want him to win." Noah's whispered words to his sister make my heart swell. He loves her so much and she isn't even here yet.

"She'll be here…" My voice trails off as a warm rush of water floods my feet.

"Eww! Mommy peed her pants!" Noah shouts, jumping away from me.

"Oh no. Oh no."

The final seconds of the half tick down as I try to breathe through the pain that is now hitting me.

This can't be happening.

"Tenley! Oh my God! Did what I think just happened, happen?" Peyton is peering down around me, looking for confirmation. Carter and Angie are right by her side.

"Umm, yes?"

"Yes or no? Not a hard question. Did your water just break?" Her voice is sharp as she pins me with a glare.

"Obviously yes. But what the heck am I supposed to do? We're in the middle of the Super Bowl!"

"I don't think she cares. Where's your mom?" Peyton springs into action as I take deep breaths.

"Baby girl is coming?" Jackson's dad walks down the row of seats, picking Noah up, who still has a horrified look on his face.

"Uh-huh." I'm rubbing my belly, now trying to breathe through a contraction.

So much for Braxton-Hicks.

"She's not supposed to be here for another few weeks."

"I guess she wants to see her dad win a Super Bowl."

"Okay," Peyton says, coming back over, "EMTs are headed up and are going to take you to the hospital. Your mom and Jackson's mom will go with you, and we'll let Jackson know—"

"No!" I shout, trying to stand. "You can't tell him until after the game. He needs to be here for his team!"

The lights go out as the field is prepped for halftime.

Damn it. I really wanted to see the Backstreet Boys.

"Are you sure?" Peyton asks.

I nod. "Yes. I want him here."

Carter comes around to the front row, extending two hands to me, helping me up. "What can we do to help?"

I lean into him, making the short distance to the waiting EMTs in the suite.

"Make sure Noah isn't too much?"

Carter smiles at me. "He can play with Angie. They'll be fine."

I try to smile, but it's more a wince. "Thank you. I hope it's not too much trouble."

"It'll be good practice for when we have two." Carter winks at me.

"Are you guys having another?" I ask as he settles me on the gurney.

"Not yet. But when we do, I'll be sure to get your advice."

Another contraction hits.

Baby girl is coming fast.

"One last time—are you sure you don't want us to tell Jackson?"

I breathe through the pain, nodding. "I'm sure."

Jackson's dad comes over with Noah. "We'll be sure to get him there in time. You worry about yourself." He squeezes my hand.

"And you, mister"—I give Noah a kiss on the cheek—"make sure to cheer extra loud for Daddy and stay with Grandpa, okay?"

Noah nods his head furiously. "Okay, Mommy! Have fun!"

The Big Game

I give him a smile as I'm wheeled out of the suite. Fun is so not the right word for what's about to happen.

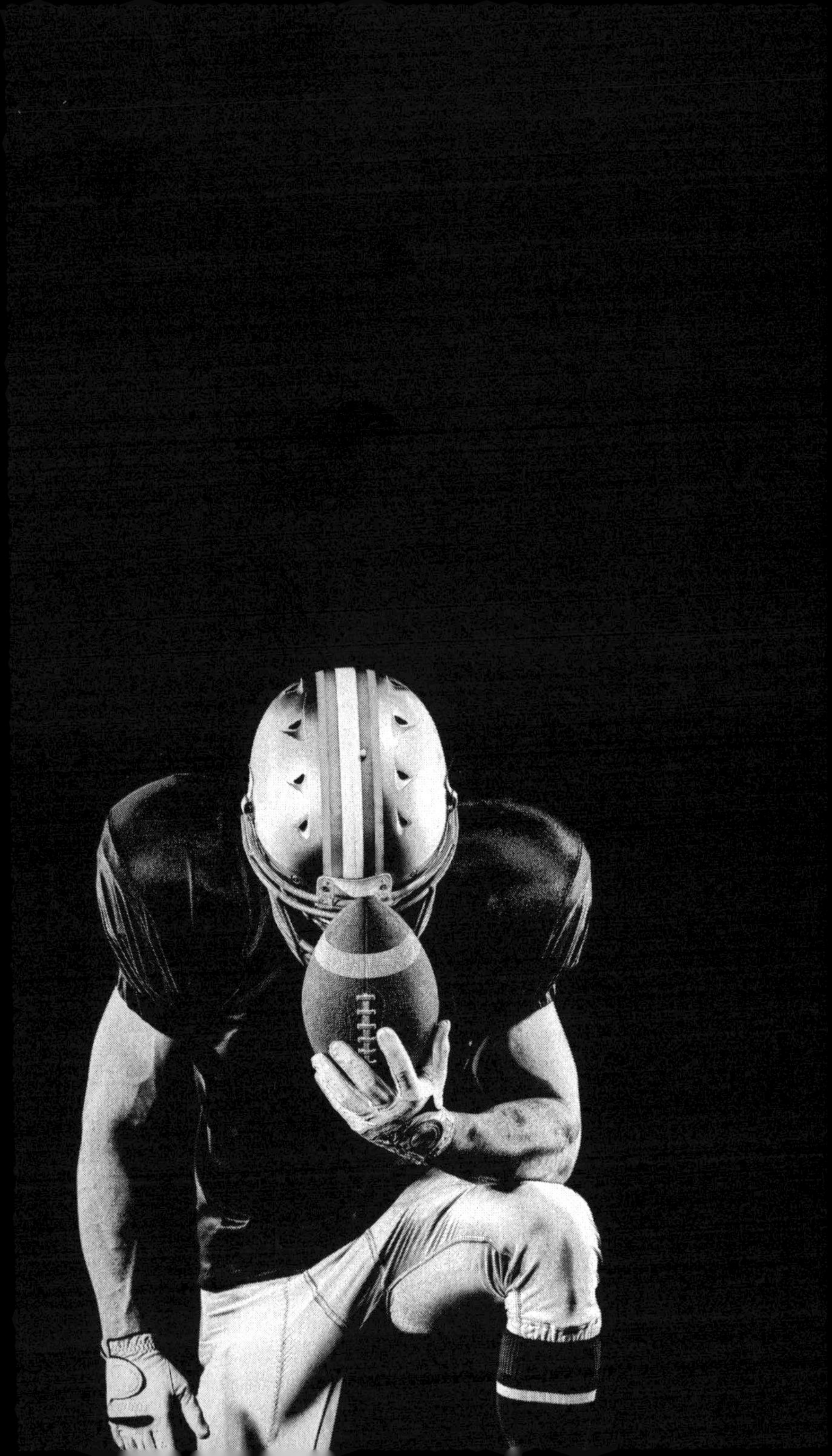

Chapter Seven

KNOX

Fuck.

Things are not going our way. After a late pick-six by LA, they're kicking our asses. In our own stadium.

Guys are beat down. We've all been playing our hearts out, but we don't have much to show for it.

If it weren't for Jackson, we'd be out of it completely.

Dejection hangs in the locker room. Half the team has their heads down while the other half looks exhausted.

The muffled music of the halftime show can be heard right now.

But I don't give a shit.

All I care about right now is that we have thirty minutes of football left.

To say we're not playing our best football right now is an understatement.

And I for one don't care for it.

"Okay, so that was a shitty first half," I say, moving to stand in the center of the locker room. A few heads pop up.

"You can say that again," someone mumbles.

"It was. But it wasn't any one person's fault. Alex"—I point to him—"what can you do better in the second half?"

"Maybe hit my targets?" he scoffs.

"Colin?" I flip my gaze over to him.

"Actually catch the passes Alex throws my way?"

I nod. "We're down by fifteen thanks to Jackson closing the gap. How many touchdowns are we down, Logan?" I look at him. He looks like this is a trick question.

"Two, plus a two-point conversion."

"Damn straight. I know I didn't play my best, but we still have thirty minutes to turn this around."

Alex stands, walking over to me and clapping me on the shoulder. "Knox is right. Game isn't over. I don't know about you guys, but I didn't come this far to roll over and give them the game. Hell no!"

The energy shifts in the locker room. Shoulders aren't dropping anymore. All eyes are on Alex and me.

"Losing sucks," Colin states as he comes over to stand next to us. "I don't want to carry a Super Bowl loss with me for the rest of my life. Because you know we will. Every single fan will remember this season. How we played the best regular season game of our life, but couldn't win the big one."

"I don't want that. You, Alex?" I ask him.

"Fuck no!" he shouts.

Guys start standing, coming into the center of the locker room. Coach Brooks is watching us, trying to hide a smile.

"First half is behind us. It's over and done. Chalk it up to nerves, bad play, whatever you want." I look around. "Second half, we show up. Clean up your routes. No dumb penalties. Let's go out there and play the Mountain Lion football that I know we're all capable of."

"James, what is it you and Peyton always do before a game?" Logan asks.

He smiles. "I tell her how many yards and the number of touchdowns I'm going to get."

"And where are you?"

"Thirty-seven yards. No touchdowns." He shakes his head before looking to Logan. "Think I can close the gap in the second half?"

Logan is vibrating. "Not if I run the ball for one hundred yards and a touchdown myself."

Alex comes between the two, wrapping his arms around them. "How about I give you each a touchdown? That'll close the gap."

Jackson pops up. "I'll throw in a couple of field goals to sweeten the deal."

I'm grinning like an idiot. This is the energy we need. "Hell, maybe I'll force a fumble in there somewhere too."

"Why don't you add a recovery to that as well?" Colin says.

"Fuck yeah! That sounds great!" I slap him on the pads. "Alright boys, bring it in!"

Everyone crowds us in the center of the room.

"Captain?" I look to Alex. He's always one for big speeches.

"This is all you, buddy." He throws his arm up, and we all follow suit.

I grin. My eyes find Frankie's on the side of the locker room. Her eyes are wet, but I don't miss the *I love you* she mouths to me.

There's no way we're losing tonight. Because that woman deserves two rings tonight—not just one.

"We can't score fifteen points in one play." I look at every player around me. "Slow and steady. One drive. One play. One stop. Play your game—smart, clean football.

This is our time. No one is going to beat us in our own house!"

"Hell no!"

"Let's win it for Denver!"

Their words give me chills. Coach steps into the center of the fold.

"Coach, bring it home."

He smiles, throwing his hand up with everyone else. "I don't know what more I can say that hasn't already been said. Go out there and play the game you love, and let's bring a championship home to Denver!"

"Family on three…" I count down.

"Family!"

Nothing is standing between us and that win.

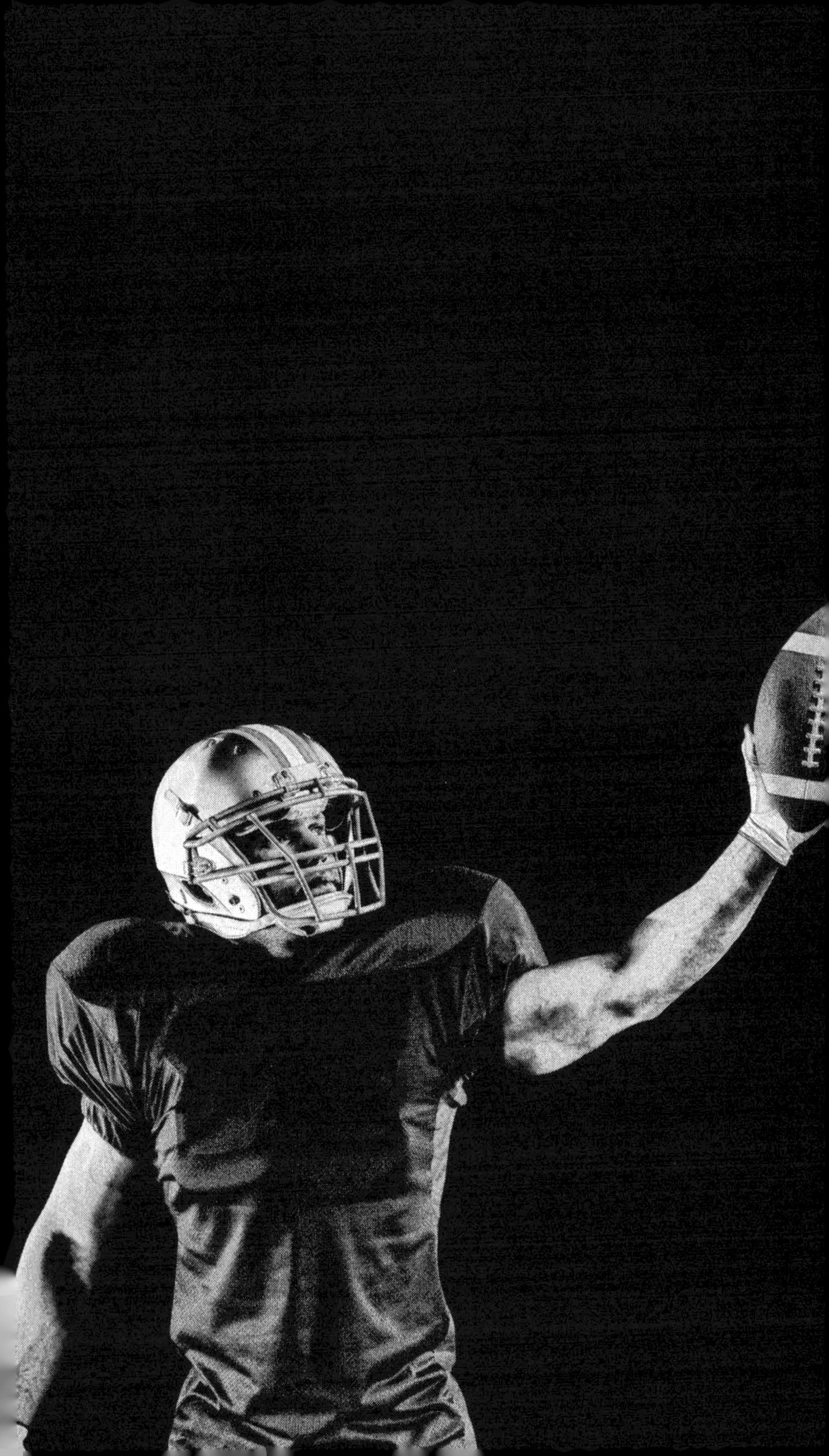

Chapter Eight

COLIN

"Alright, boys. This is it. Ten yards and we're in the lead. Think we can pull it off?" Alex asks in the huddle, looking every single one of us in the eye.

There's a minute left on the clock. We're down by three points. After being down by eighteen at one point, no one thought we would be here. We've fought tooth and nail to get into this position.

34-31.

To win the fucking Super Bowl.

"Let's fucking go." I clap him on the shoulder.

"Rodgers. You ready?" Alex asks our backup running back.

Logan went down in the third quarter after a bad hit to his leg. Getting carted off the field in the Super Bowl isn't what anyone wants.

But he helped get us into this position right now.

"Ready, Alex."

Alex calls the play and we line up. Our offensive line pushes the defense back as Rodgers runs for three.

Another running play.

This time for four yards.

"Three yards. Colin, you're up."

You could see my smile from space. "Let's do it, Alex."

"Blackbird Thirty-two on three."

We break the huddle and I run to my spot. The safety across from me is the one Peyton made me watch over and over again.

And then one more time just to make sure it sank in.

Cut to the right to beat him.

The ball is snapped and I dart toward the middle of the field. Just when I think he has me beat, I cut to the right. He goes left and the perfect spiral sails right into my hands.

"Touchdown. Number Eighty-Seven. Wide Receiver Colin James," comes the voice over the speakers in the stadium.

"Best fucking pass of your life!" I jump into Alex's arms as what feels like half the team swarms me in the end zone.

"Best fucking catch of your life!" Alex echoes back. "We're in the lead!"

Jackson jogs onto the field, bypassing all of us to stay in the zone. One extra point later, we're up 38-34.

With thirty-four seconds left on the clock.

"Alright, boys. Don't give them one yard. Not one single fucking yard!" Knox is walking up and down the sideline, hyping up the defense. I'm standing on top of the bench next to Alex, my heart in my throat.

The ball is kicked off and LA's special team kick returner watches the ball sail over his head through the end zone.

"I can't watch." Alex is twisting his hands together, staring at the ground. Everyone in the stadium is on their feet.

The Big Game

There are more Mountain Lions' fans than LA fans, so it's loud. Not like we're used to, but the energy is in our favor.

They get an easy five yards on the first play, but the clock doesn't stop. Neither team has a time-out. LA is quick to the line.

The ball is snapped and it happens in slow motion. Knox beats the guard and gets to their quarterback. The ball is fumbled and it's chaos on the field.

"Get the ball! Get the ball!" I'm shouting like a lunatic, not that it'll make any difference.

"Who has it?" Alex is squeezing my shoulder, watching the screen. "Who has the ball?"

Bodies are being pulled off the pile as the refs try to find the ball. And when they do, it's our guy coming up with it. The ball is in Knox fucking Fisher's hand.

Denver ball.

The clock winds down to zero.

Game over.

The Denver Mountain Lions are Super Bowl champions.

"Holy crap!" I tackle Alex to the ground. "We did it! We fucking did it!"

"We did it!" We're both crying as cannons shoot confetti over the field.

"Got room in that hug for me?" Knox is at our side, dropping his helmet.

"MVP, right here!" I jump up to hug him as Alex does the same.

"That was the play of the year," Alex agrees.

"Nah. That pass was pretty great."

"Not as great as my catch."

"Agree to disagree," Alex says as Jackson joins the fray.

"Motherfucking champions, baby!" Tears are wet on

his face. We're all crying and not a single person cares. Championship hats are given to each of us as a stage is starting to be constructed on the field.

"I love you guys." Alex is choked up. "I can't believe we finally won!"

"We did it!" Jackson chirps.

"Fucking champs!" Knox shouts.

As families start coming out onto the field, we break apart, finding our loved ones. It should hurt more that my dad isn't here, but it doesn't. Even after all these years, he still hasn't reached out to mend fences.

But because of the woman coming toward me, I'm okay. And I'll always be okay.

She stops in front of me, her hands tucked into the back pockets of her jeans. She's looking as sexy as ever in her eighty-seven jersey.

"Only ninety-seven yards, James? And one touchdown? I'm disappointed in you." She's fighting a smile.

"I'm hoping the fact that it was the game-winning touchdown will make up for the three yards and one touchdown I didn't get."

Peyton shrugs a shoulder before launching herself into my arms. "You bet your ass it does! I am so proud of you. You won. Oh my God, you did it!" She's peppering my face with kisses. Her face is as wet as mine.

"We did it. I can't believe we pulled that off!"

"Do you think next time you can maybe make it a bit easier on us?"

I drop my hat onto her head, twisting it backward so I can see her face.

"It's not like we wanted it to be that hard."

Peyton wraps her arms around my neck, dropping her forehead to mine. "Aren't you glad we watched all that film?"

My grin is a mile wide. "You know what that means, right?"

"I know." Her smile matches my own.

"Every Super Bowl here on out, you and me. Watching film."

"Deal."

Peyton and football.

It's all I'll ever need.

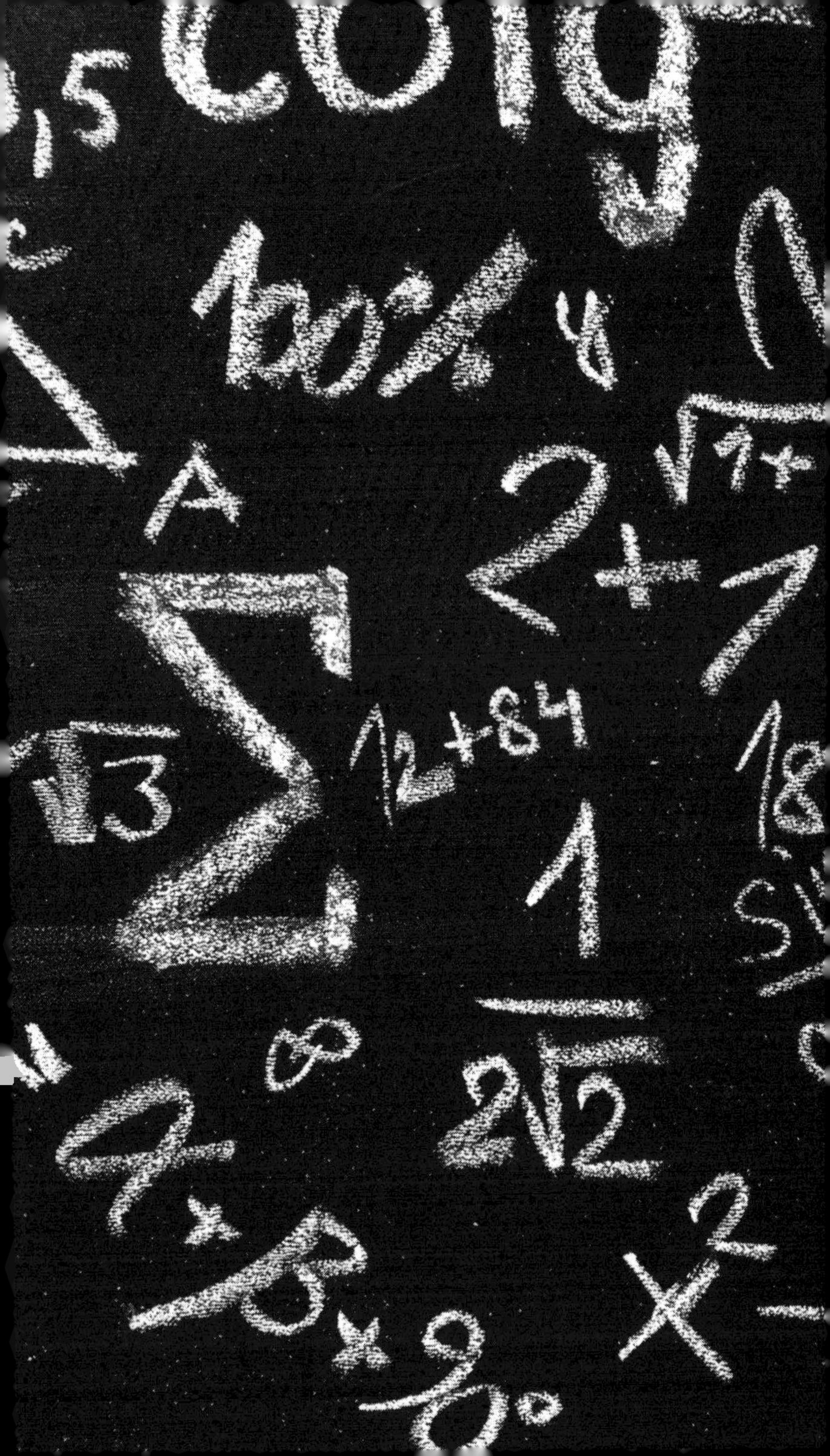

Chapter Nine

CARTER

"I can't believe they won!" Tommy slaps me on the shoulder as everyone in the family suite prepares to go down onto the field. "I didn't think they could do it."

"I knew Daddy would win, Uncle Tommy." Angie's face is fierce as she turns it on him. It's quite the change in tune from when she was almost in tears not twenty minutes ago. Thank God they won.

"You're right, munchkin. What do you say we go see him?"

Her face is bright as she jumps into my arms. "We can see him now?"

I nod. "Yes. But you have to stay with one of us, okay? There's going to be a lot of people down there."

She nods, taking my face in her tiny hands. "Guess what, Papa?"

"What?"

"Daddy won the Super Bowl!"

My grin matches hers. "Daddy won the Super Bowl!"

Angie turns to Tommy as the elevator arrives. "Guess what, Uncle Tommy?"

He gives her his best thinking look. "Did Daddy win the Super Bowl?"

She shouts, throwing her arms up into the air. "Daddy won the Super Bowl!"

Everyone is beaming with pride as we make our way through the stadium. My mom is crying, heading to see my dad. Alex's parents still have tears streaming down their faces.

It's been a long road. There were days I wondered if we'd ever get here.

But here we are.

I never imagined this is where Alex and I would be five years ago. He was scared to live his truth, and I wouldn't go back into the closet for him. But since he came out, we've been by each other's side every day. Marriage. Kids. I never expected any of it with Alex, but the life we've created is better than anything I thought possible.

It's pure chaos as we make our way onto the field. Confetti cannons are still going off, and players are running around congratulating each other. Angie's in my arms, trying to catch all the confetti she can. I set her on the ground, trying to find Alex.

"Papa! The confetti is Denver colors!" Nothing exists for her except trying to shove as much confetti as she can in her coat pockets.

Jackson goes racing by us, no doubt having been told the news about Tenley. It's then my eyes find Alex. The quarterback coach is congratulating him as our eyes lock. My heart stutters in my chest. I can feel his happiness from here. His smile is as bright as I've ever seen it.

I squat down, getting on Angie's level. "Want to see Daddy?"

Her eyes pop up, searching around me. "Where is he?" I point to where he's standing, and her eyes go wide, excited at seeing one of her favorite people in the world. She takes off running. For a four-year-old, she's fast. Confetti is flying out of her pockets in her wake.

Alex is waiting with open arms as he lifts her in the air. "You won, Daddy!" Her tiny arms are squeezing his neck when I make it over to them.

"We won." His voice is shaky as I wrap my arms around them. Life hasn't ever been better than it is right now. But I also know it's about to get a lot better.

Alex

LIFE COULDN'T BE BETTER. With Angie and Carter in my arms and confetti raining down on us, it's pretty damn perfect. The second I saw them on the field, I got choked up. But with them in my arms, it's hard to hold back the tears.

"You did it." Carter squeezes me closer to him. I bury my face in his neck, letting the tears fall. "You won the Super Bowl!"

Pride drips from his voice.

"I can't believe we did it."

Carter pulls back, cupping my cheeks in his hands. "That was the best game of football I've ever seen."

I can't help but laugh at him. Just a few short years ago, he wanted nothing to do with jocks or football. But now he's teaching Angie as much about the game as I am.

"You about gave me a heart attack!"

"Maybe we'll make the next one easier."

Carter smiles back at me. "I like the sound of that."

"Can you play in the Super Bowl next year, Daddy?" Angie asks.

"We'll see. We have to make it there."

"You will. You're the best football player EVER! I love you so much, Daddy."

I squeeze her closer to me. If only every analyst said this about me. There's nothing like being this girl's daddy.

"Not as much as I love you." The tears are coming again as my parents and Tommy come into view.

"Nice win, bro," Tommy says, tongue-in-cheek.

I roll my eyes at him. "Thanks. Glad I impressed you."

"Don't listen to him," Dad says, clapping me on the shoulder. "That was a hell of a game, son. We are so proud of you."

Carter takes Angie from me, so I can hug them both. I'm at a loss for words. There is so much love right now that I don't know what to do with myself.

"Just had to go for the comeback, didn't you?" Tommy teases.

"Hey, we won, right?"

Mom is crying and Angie is back on the ground, making snow angels in the confetti. There's nothing better than seeing the joy on my daughter's face. Carter is looking at me like I hung the moon.

"That last drive? I thought I was going to puke. I don't know how you do it." Tommy pulls me in for a hug.

I hug him back. I don't know if I'd be where I am now if it weren't for his support. "I'm glad you were here to see it."

"Nowhere else I'd be. I love you, Alex." He pulls back, wiping a tear from his eye.

"You two are going to get me started again," Mom says, the tears still streaming down her face.

Wiping my own tears off my face, I turn to her and

pull her in for a hug. "I don't think you ever stopped, Mom."

"Oh hush." She swats at me.

"Alex. They're getting ready to present the trophy. We need you up on stage." I nod to the team staffer who's appeared at my side and let go of my mom.

"Angie. You ready to go get that trophy?"

"Can I hold it?" she asks. I dip down, lifting her up onto my shoulders.

"After everyone else gets their turn."

She pats me on the head, telling me to get going as we head that way.

"I'm going, I'm going."

All the guys are gathered around the stage, except one. "Where's Jackson?"

Carter stops me amid the chaos. "No one told you?"

"No. What happened?"

Carter is beaming. "She went into labor."

"No way."

Angie tilts my head up to look at her. "Will I get a baby sister like Noah?"

"Uhh…"

"How about we talk about that later, sweetheart?" Carter cuts me off. Thank God.

She just shrugs her shoulders as we make it to the stage. Coach is there to greet us.

"Grandpa! We won! We won the Super Bowl."

At this point, I'm not sure who's more excited—me or Angie.

"All because of your dad." He claps me on the shoulder. My eyes are wet again. It seems it's going to be a night of endless tears.

"I couldn't have done it without you, Coach."

"Nah, I think you could have. But what do you say? Let's go get that trophy, Mr. MVP."

"Are you serious?" Carter asks beside me.

He nods. "After that comeback in the second half? He more than deserves it."

Carter hugs his dad before I pull him in for another hug, awkward with Angie still sitting on my shoulders.

"Does that mean you're the best player, Daddy?" Angie asks from her perch.

I go to answer, but Coach cuts me off. "It does. And don't let him tell you otherwise. C'mere and give Grandpa a hug."

He pulls Angie off my shoulders, taking her with him up on stage.

"This doesn't feel real," I say so only Carter can hear me.

"You'll probably get sick of hearing this, but I'm so proud of you. The strength it took to come back like that?" Carter's eyes are wet now. "Not many people could do it, Alex. But you did. I love you so damn much and can't wait to celebrate with you. Only you."

I pull him in for a kiss, one that is too short. "I will never get sick of hearing that."

"Good, because I'm never going to stop saying it. Now,"—Carter pushes me toward the stage—"go get that trophy."

Music to my ears.

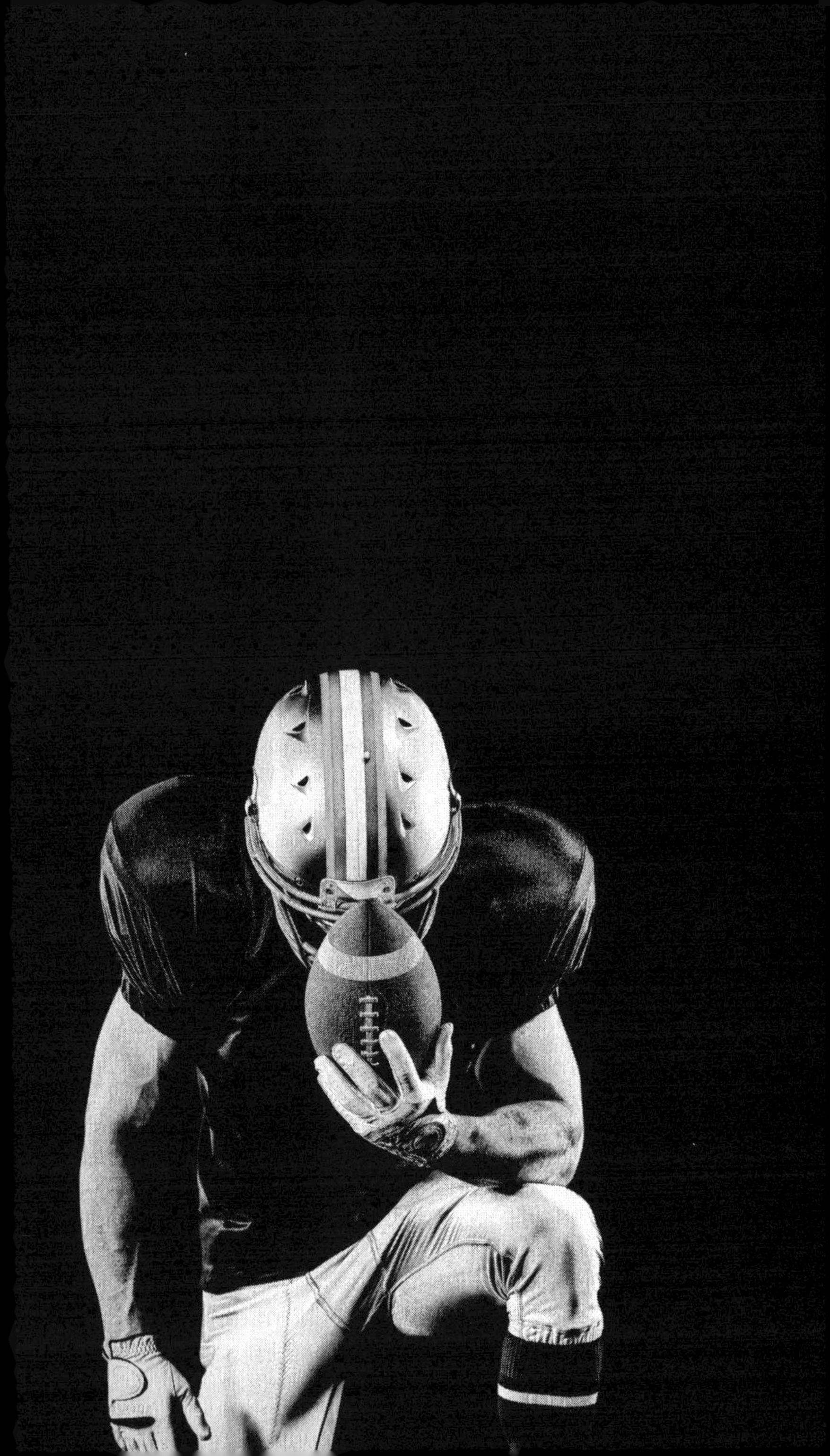

Chapter Ten

KNOX

"I can't believe you did it!" Frankie leaps into my arms. Confetti covers the field as I hold her to me. "That was the best damn play I've ever seen."

"All because of you." I bury my face in her neck. "I wouldn't be half the player I am if it weren't for you."

Frankie looks down at me, her hair tucked beneath the team beanie. It's cold, but not as cold as it could be.

"We won this together. How many people can say that?"

I squeeze her closer to me. It was an adjustment not having Frankie as my coach. It was much better than the alternative of her going elsewhere though. There's no way I'd be standing here right now if not for the woman I'm holding.

"I love you, Frankie."

"Not as much as I love you."

I lay one on her, not caring who's around us. I'm sure this moment is being memorialized by the dozens of photographers on the field.

Hopefully someone will send me a copy.

Because life couldn't get any better than this.

"Can you spare a minute to say hi to your mother?"

Pulling away from Frankie, I see my mom standing beside me in my jersey, her eyes red from crying.

"Hi, Mom."

I pull her in for a bone-crushing hug.

"I am so proud of you." Her voice starts to shake again. "Your grandparents would be too."

That gets the tears going again. If there's anything that could make this victory sweeter, it would be to have my grandparents here.

Having the support of the two most important people in my life, and having them by my side right now is pretty damn special.

"I'm a Super Bowl champion."

I step back, trying to take a calming breath. Frankie is just as emotional as she hugs my mom. The two have been thick as thieves since they met.

"The first woman to win a Super Bowl as a coach. Pretty badass, dear." Mom pats Frankie's cheek. I'm not sure who is bursting with more pride—me or Frankie.

"That's got a great ring to it," she tells me, turning to face me.

"Speaking of rings…" I trail off, watching a range of emotions cross Frankie's face. "Are you going to let me do it now?"

She rolls those big brown eyes at me. "If you must."

Sticking my hand out toward Mom, she drops the small velvet pouch in my palm.

"So that's where you've been hiding it this week." A grin spreads across Frankie's face.

"You didn't actually think I was going to propose last night, did you?"

She gives me a pondering look. "It did cross my mind."

The Big Game

"Well,"—I grab one of her hands as I sink to one knee—"I happened to know we'd win today and could do it now."

"You knew we were going to win after being down by eighteen?" Only Frankie would get sidetracked during a proposal by football talk.

"Gran wouldn't let us lose. She'd haunt me until my dying day if I did."

Both my mom and Frankie laugh at that. "Very true."

"Now, do you mind if I get back to the matter at hand?" I squeeze her hand in mine.

"I wish you would."

This woman. Like I'm the one being distracted.

"Since the day I first met you, Francesca, you've been a powerhouse in my life. You don't take any shit from me—"

"Must you cuss in your proposal?" Mom rolls her eyes at me.

"Would you two stop interrupting me and let me do the damn thing?"

Both of them fight a laugh as Frankie nods at me to continue.

"Is this really what I have to look forward to the rest of my life?" I mutter to myself.

"Yes. And you wouldn't want it any other way." Frankie is glowing in the lights of the field. Out of the corner of my eye, I see a photographer with a camera aimed in our direction.

"You're right. You keep me on my toes. You never let me get away with anything. If it weren't for you, I wouldn't be the man or the player I am today. You are the best thing that has ever happened to me, Frankie, and I don't ever want to spend a minute of my life without you."

"Much better, Knox," Mom whispers, giving me a thumbs-up.

I smile at her before turning my attention back to Frankie. I pull Grandma's ring out of the pouch. The small round diamond is set between two smaller diamonds. It's simple, but full of love.

"Francesca Rose, would you do me the honor of marrying me and letting me spend the rest of my life showering you in love?"

"Hell yes!" Frankie cheers, throwing herself at me.

Mom claps as Frankie takes my face in her hands and lays one on me. The last of the confetti sticks to our faces as we bask in this moment.

I slide the ring down Frankie's finger, and it's fucking perfect on her hand. I know my grandparents would have loved to experience this moment, seeing her wearing this ring. But I know they're watching me.

Frankie sits on my knee, hugging me to her. "I love you, Knox."

"I love you, Frankie." I take her hand, kissing the ring. "Where does this ring fall in the rings you've gotten tonight?"

She gives me the brightest smile yet. One that tells me that winning the Super Bowl doesn't hold a candle to this moment.

"Best ring I'll ever get in my life."

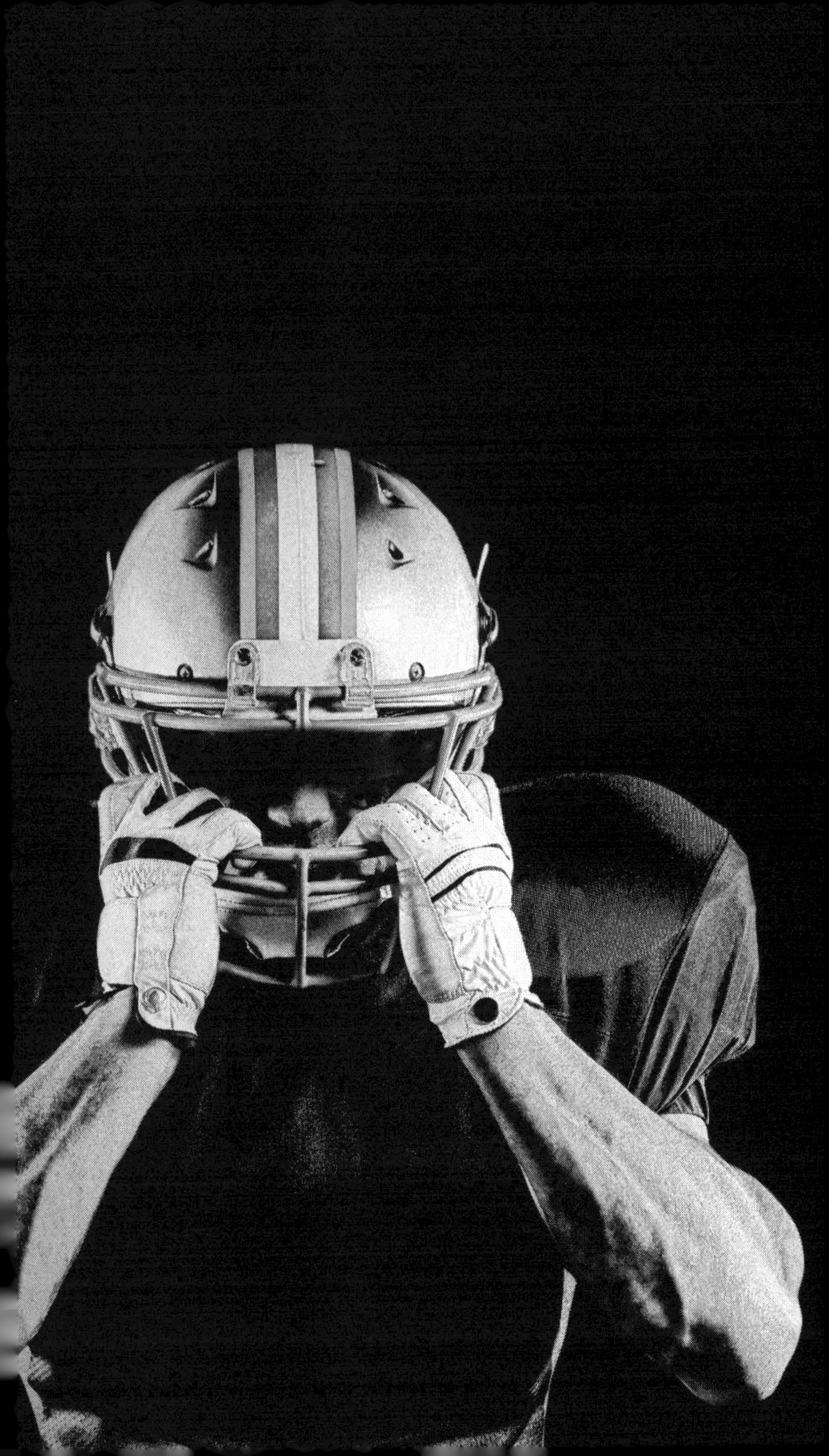

Chapter Eleven

JACKSON

"Holy shit! We did it!" Confetti pours down around us as Knox jumps onto my back. "Can you believe it?"

"That forced fumble was fucking insane, man!" The last play of the game was nothing short of heroic. Nothing like winning a Super Bowl in your own stadium.

"We're world champions!" He runs off as I finally see my dad and Noah with Colin and Peyton on the sidelines.

The closer I get, the more excited Noah is, squirming in my dad's arms.

"Can you believe we won?" I shout, taking him in my arms.

His tiny arms wrap around my neck. "Mommy peed her pants during the game!"

"What?" My confused face finds my dad. His hands are up, as if I won't like what he's telling me.

"She went into labor."

"She what? The doctor said she was fine for another few weeks." I couldn't have heard that right, but my dad is grinning from ear to ear and nodding his head. "We still have a few weeks."

It's like if I keep saying it, it'll stop it from happening.

"Babies don't operate on schedule, son."

The field is packed. Players, families, friends, and reporters are everywhere.

"Are you serious?" I look at Noah, as if his tiny face will confirm what my dad is telling me.

"Both moms are there, but things are moving fast," Dad tells me.

"The baby's not here yet? Crap. I need to get there."

My dad grabs Noah out of my arms as I pat my pants for my keys. "Shit! How am I going to get there?"

"Swear jar, Daddy!"

"Jackson, deep breath." Peyton comes up next to me, with Colin staring at me like he can't believe what is happening.

"How am I supposed to get to the fucking hospital?" I shout, spinning around. I'm losing my mind trying to figure out how to get there.

"Another dollar!"

"Now's not the time, Noah," my dad says to him.

"There's a sheriff at the end of the tunnel ready to take you to the hospital. Your dad will bring Noah later, but right now,"—she slaps a hat on my head—"you need to go see your baby girl enter the world."

"You're the best." I give her a quick hug before turning and giving Noah a kiss. "I'll see you real soon, bud, and then we can celebrate."

"Yay!" He pumps his fists in the air as my dad slaps me on the back.

"Go! That baby is coming fast."

The smile that bursts out on my face is huge as I run in

the direction Peyton points me in. I ignore everyone in my way as I find a beaming police officer waiting for me.

"Looks like one of our champs needs a ride to the hospital?"

"Fast as you can."

"Don't worry, we'll get you there quickly."

―――

"DID I MISS IT?" I burst into the delivery room and all eyes turn to face me. Tenley lets out a huge scream as my mom waves me over.

"She's almost here," the doctor says.

"You won!" Tenley has tears streaming down her face as I grab her hand and drop a kiss onto her sweaty forehead.

"And yet, winning the Super Bowl isn't the most exciting thing happening tonight."

The city was electric as we raced here. People were pouring into the streets to celebrate Denver's win. It was years in the making, and I couldn't have been more excited until now.

"One more push and she'll be out," the doctor pipes up.

"You've got this, Tenley."

Squeezing my hand, she starts pushing until the best sound I've heard all night hits my ears.

"She's here!" The doctor holds up a tiny baby girl, covered in goo and screaming her head off.

Tears leak out of my eyes as she's set on Tenley's chest.

"I guess you didn't want to miss out on all the fun, did you?" Tenley strokes a finger down her chubby cheek.

"She looks just like you," I whisper. I'm in awe of this tiny human that my wife just gave birth to.

Piper Fields.

"We'll get her cleaned up for you and then you can get back to your room to rest." A nurse takes her from Tenley as she turns to face me, eyes glistening with happiness.

"I can't believe she was early."

I nod. "I was told you peed your pants at the game."

A laugh escapes Tenley's lips as I settle on the bed next to her. "Noah will eventually learn."

Cupping her cheek, I bring her gaze up to meet mine. "I am so proud of you, Tenley."

"I love you." Her words are whispered as I lean down to kiss her.

"Love of my fucking life."

Her lips smile against mine. "Swear jar."

"You're just as bad as Noah." I laugh.

"You want to hold her, Dad?" The nurse brings the now quiet bundle over.

"I didn't think I'd make it." I don't take my eyes off Piper's as she's placed in my arms. It feels like my heart just grew three sizes.

"I'm so glad you did."

Hospital staff are moving all around us, but I don't notice a thing. Our moms are hovering, watching us love on our baby girl.

"Are you ready to head back to your room?" The nurse appears at my side and asks Tenley.

"Your dad and Noah are in the waiting room," my mom says next to me.

"Noah has to be exhausted," Tenley says on a yawn. The woman just birthed a human and she's worried about our son. One of the endless reasons I love her.

The Big Game

I lean down, taking her lips in a long kiss. "Don't worry. I'll take care of him tomorrow."

"Don't you have a Super Bowl you should be celebrating?"

I shrug a shoulder. "It can wait."

"KNOCK, KNOCK. GOT ROOM FOR A VISITOR?"

Coach's head pops into the room. I glance over at Tenley, sleeping with her arms wrapped around Noah.

"Thought the little lady might want to see what all the fuss was about since she got here early."

He pulls the Super Bowl trophy from behind his back. I shift the sleeping bundle on my chest. Thankfully I was able to clean up in the hospital shower, because all I want to do now is cuddle this baby girl.

"Wow. How'd you manage to get this out of the afterparty?" It's early Monday morning and I know some of my teammates are still out celebrating.

"I appealed to their good side."

"You mean they were too drunk to notice?"

He laughs. "That too."

Coach passes the trophy over, all seven pounds equally balancing out the best thing to be placed in my arms all night.

I can't believe we did it. It hasn't sunk in. I rushed out of that stadium so fast, I didn't even think what the moment meant. My dad had to bring me the Super Bowl T-shirt I'm wearing now. I peek over at the bed, and Tenley's eyes are now on me, filled with tears.

I still remember when I thought my life had no meaning if I never won this trophy. But now, looking between the trophy and my baby girl, there's no contest which one wins. The small baby girl has my entire heart. I never knew my heart could live outside my chest once. Let alone three times.

"Thanks, Coach. This means a lot." I hear the click of a camera and see him smiling as he holds his phone up.

"Fatherhood looks good on you. I'm proud of you, Jackson."

I set the trophy down, nodding back to him. "Kind of makes you wish you could smack younger me out of wasting so many years of my life."

He just shrugs. "Yeah, but without them, would you appreciate all this?"

My gaze finds Tenley's again. I don't know what I would do without her. She's been my everything for as long as I can remember—before I even knew it. Without her, I wouldn't have this tiny bundle of joy in my arms. I wouldn't have the crazy ball of energy that's sleeping in her arms.

"I don't think I would."

This win will be forever.

A forever that I get to spend celebrating with my family at my side.

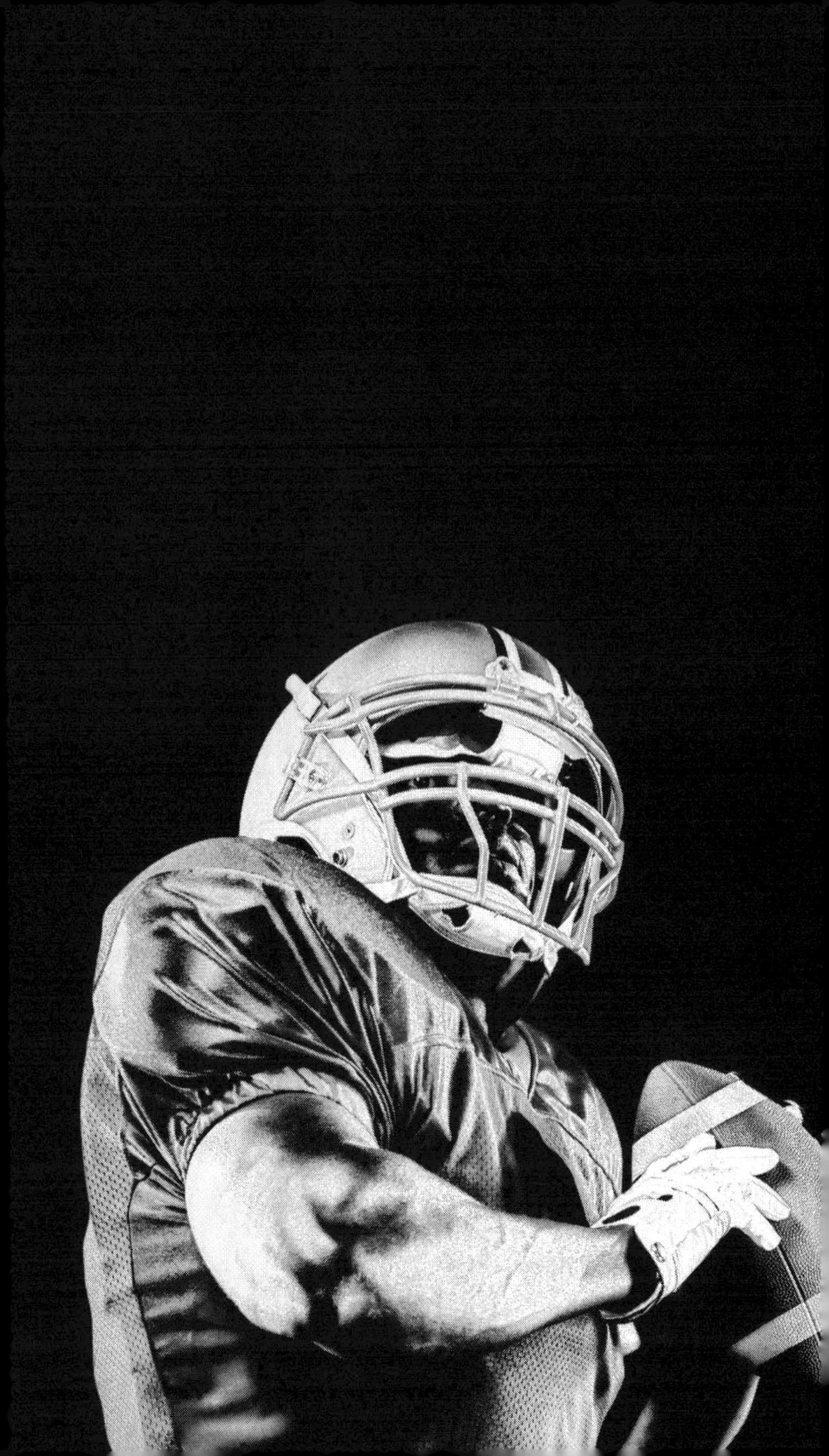

Chapter Twelve

ALEX

"I can't believe we won the Super Bowl." The overhead lights are flashing in the bar we're sitting in that's attached to the hotel. They shut everything down for the team. Champagne has been flowing all night. Guys are dancing on the dance floor, celebrating with loved ones.

"You are Super Bowl MVP," Carter shouts back at me.

"I still can't believe it." I wrap an arm around Carter's shoulders, dropping kisses up and down his neck. "We won the Super Bowl!"

Carter's beaming as he turns toward me, brushing a stray lock of hair off my forehead. "I am so proud of you, Alex. I know these last few years haven't been easy, but you did it."

My emotions have been all over the place tonight. One minute I'm fine, the next I'm crying again. I pull Carter in for a hug, because it's about the only thing that will keep me from losing it. Again.

Something Angie had no problem pointing out when I cried when I was named MVP.

"Will you two get a room? You're as bad as Colin and Peyton," Knox shouts from across the table.

"You have no room to talk," I laugh, wiping away a stray tear. I stay curled into Carter's side. "I couldn't pry you away from Frankie if I tried."

Knox shrugs a shoulder. "It's what happens when she finally let me propose to her."

Frankie smacks him across the chest. "You make it sound like I didn't want you to propose."

"I would've proposed three fucking years ago if it were up to me."

"Are you ready to get out of here?" Carter whispers against my neck as the two start bickering over who wanted to get married first. "I love your teammates and all, but I'm ready to get you alone."

"Knox. Frankie." I stand, waving at both of them.

"Finally! Took ya long enough," Knox says, winking at me.

"Might I suggest taking your own advice?" Frankie is tightly pressed against his side, just like I was to Carter not a minute ago. "No one needs to get arrested for public indecency tonight."

"Don't worry about us. Take care of your man."

Carter pulls me away before I can say another word. The music is thumping as we make our way into the lobby. It's quiet, well into Monday morning. A few security guards are floating around, but that's it.

We don't wait long for the elevator. Carter tugs me in after him, hitting the button for the top floor. "It's been way too long since I've had you all to myself."

The moment the doors are closed, he's on me. God, I missed the feel of him against me. His lips. His arms wrapped around me as we fall asleep each night.

I deepen the kiss, our tongues tangling. Each stroke has me hardening.

"You know, we might be arrested if we're not careful." My voice is laced with need as Carter kisses down my neck.

"Maybe next time you're in the Super Bowl, I'll have to sneak into your room then. I really don't like you being away from me for so long."

Carter pulls back at the ding of the elevator. His face is flushed and his lips are swollen from kissing me. Linking my hands around his back, I walk us out of the elevator. "Then we best get to the room."

Carter gives me a sinful smile.

"Seriously, you aren't helping my case here."

"Then show me some moves, Mr. MVP."

"I really like the sound of that."

"Oh yeah?" Carter quirks a brow, turning to enter our room. "Maybe I'll even give you the MVP treatment tonight."

I'm fully hard by the time Carter gets the door open and pulls me in behind him.

We shed our clothes, falling into the bathroom walk-in shower in a mess of hands and kisses as we're all over each other once again. A week was far too long without having this man inside me. I relish every second as the heat billows around us as we come together.

It's the perfect ending to a perfect day.

Something I never thought I'd ever get to experience.

"I've got some good news." Carter sits on the bed, crossing his legs. I flop down next to him. His glasses are still a bit foggy from the heat of the bathroom.

"I don't know how this day could get any better." I grab his hand, fiddling with the wedding band that rests there. It's a habit I don't think I'll ever break.

Carter's eyes tear up as he looks at me, happiness radiating out of him. "What if I told you our lives were about to get much, much better in about, oh, say seven months?"

"I must still be buzzed, because there's no way you said what I think you said."

"You heard me. Chelsea is pregnant."

"Holy shit!" I tackle Carter to the bed. "You're serious?"

He nods, wrapping himself around me. "She called Friday. The first test was a false negative."

"Oh my God." Tears are once again welling in my eyes. "We're having another baby!"

"So next time Angie asks if she's getting a sibling, we can tell her yes."

I lay one on Carter, a kiss that takes my own breath away.

"I can't believe this is my life," I whisper, seeing Carter's own happiness reflected in his bright blue eyes.

"It is pretty great," he agrees.

Never in a million years did I think I'd be here. Celebrating the Super Bowl as an out athlete with my husband and daughter with another baby on the way.

"Everything about today is perfect. I don't know if anything will ever compete with it."

"And to think, I fell in love with a football player."

I smile, peppering his face with kisses. "Thank God you did. Now, can we get back to celebrating?"

"Whatever you want, Mr. MVP."

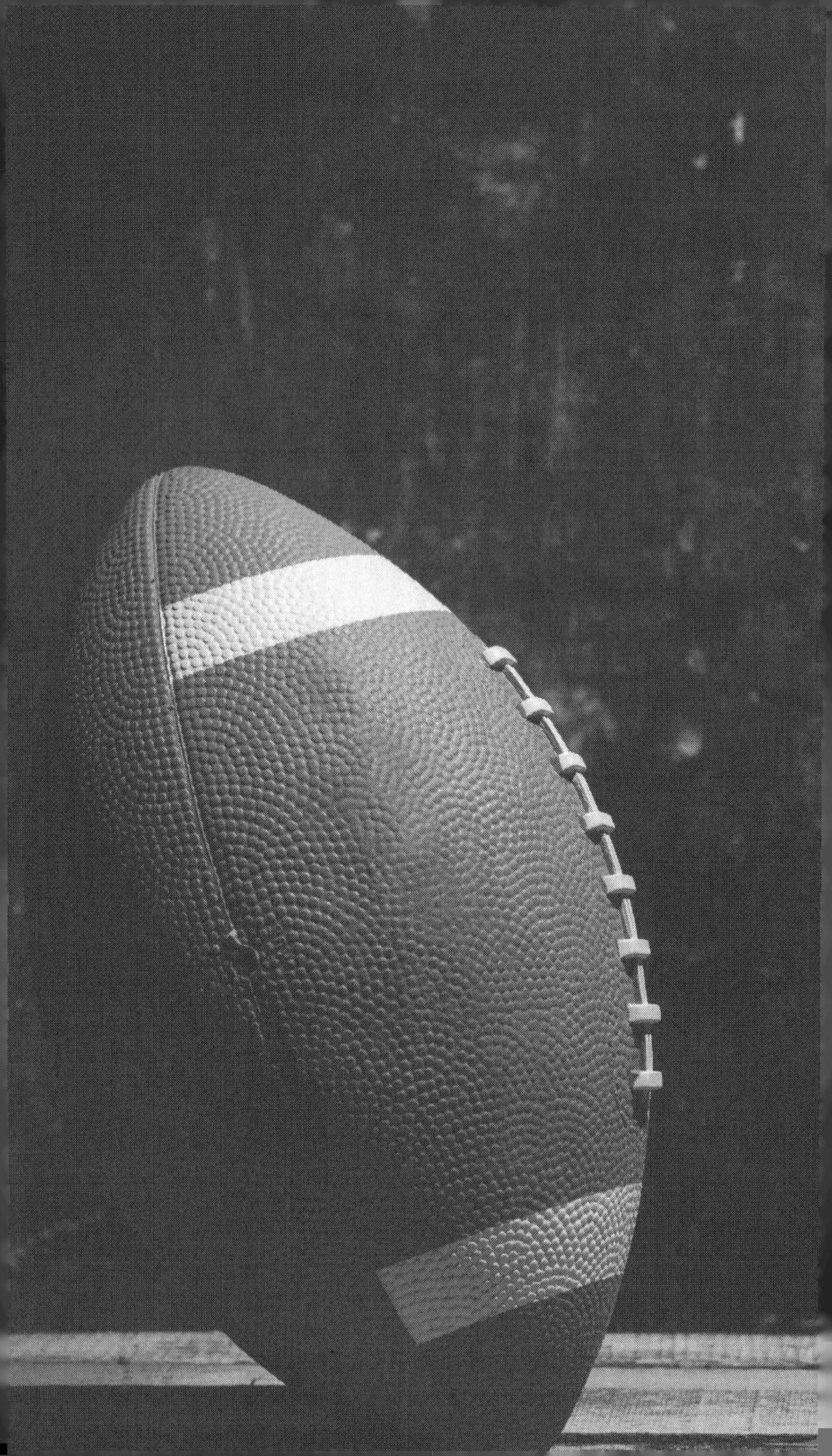

Chapter Thirteen

COACH BROOKS

It's hard to believe that at this time just a few short weeks ago we were lifting the Lombardi trophy. Now, the players who are still in town after the season ended are gathering at my house for another little celebration of sorts.

"Are you sure you want to do this?" Lexi asks from next to me. "No announcements have been made yet."

I smile back at her. "I'm sure. It's time."

My wife wraps her arms around me. "I'm proud of you. It's been a good career."

"And no better way to go out than on top."

"How do you think they'll take it?" She nods to where everyone is crowded in the living room.

I shrug my shoulders. "We'll see."

Taking her hand in mine, I follow the voices to share my news. Angie and Noah are chasing each other while their parents look on. Colin and Knox are joking around with Peyton and Frankie.

This is what I'm going to miss. Not the games or winning or hoisting the trophy.

The camaraderie of the team. The family atmosphere.

I love this team, but I'm ready for the next chapter in my life.

"Before the evening gets started, I want to say a quick few words."

Everyone quiets down immediately—no different from any day at practice.

"How's Logan, Coach?" Alex asks.

"Doc says they have everything under control. Hopefully he'll be going home next week."

I feel the collective sigh of relief. His injury has been hard, and I'm about the only person he's talked to.

"Thank God."

"I've talked to him and he seems to be in good spirits. I've told him we're all thinking of him."

"Good. Sorry to interrupt," Alex says.

"No apology necessary." I take a minute to look at each face. Now that the moment is here, it's a lot harder to get the words out. "I could not be prouder of this team. We've faced adversity through the years, but it made our victory that much sweeter."

Smiling faces stare back at me.

"While I'm proud of what we've accomplished as a team, I'm even more proud of the men you've become. That far outweighs anything we've done on the field."

Seeing how far they've come is one of the greatest joys of coaching. They are no longer boys playing a game and trying to learn about life from me. They are good men and partners who happen to play football. "And because I respect the hell out of each and every one of you, I wanted you to be the first to know. I'm retiring."

It's so quiet, you could hear a pin drop. Stunned expressions stare back at me. A squeeze of my hand tells me to keep going.

The Big Game

"I've been around this game most of my life. It's given everything to me, and I hope I'll leave the game in a better place than when I found it. But I want to spend time with my family. With my grandkids."

"That's me!" Angie's voice sounds from where Alex is now holding her.

"That's right, sweetheart." I give her a big smile.

"Wait, so who's going to be taking over?" Knox pipes up.

"The announcement will be going out in a few days. Coach Jenkins will be taking the reins."

"What does that mean for the rest of the defense?" Knox asks.

"They'll be making some moves, but rest assured, I'll be leaving you in capable hands." My gaze shifts to Frankie. "We're also in the market for a new defensive coordinator."

She straightens in Knox's arms. "Who's going to be taking over?"

"My last duty as head coach. I get to be the one to give you the good news. GM is hoping you would take over."

"Are you serious?" Shocked doesn't even begin to describe the look on her face.

"You've more than earned it, Frankie. The way you stayed cool during the big game and not let it get to you that we were down, well, that's something not a lot of people could have done. The Mountain Lions are lucky to have you. What do you say?"

"Holy shit! Yes!" She comes to me and wraps her arms around me. "I never thought this day would come!"

"It's long overdue. I'm just glad I got to be the one to tell you."

Frankie's eyes well up. "I learned from the best. Thanks for taking a chance on me all those years ago."

"It's been a rocky road, but I know you'll do great things, Frankie." She's more than proven herself these last few years after missing out on her first promotion. I know she'll be a head coach in a few years.

She runs back to Knox, leaping into his arms. He's beaming.

"Coach, mind if I say a few words?" Alex asks.

I smile at my son-in-law. "Floor is yours."

He shifts Angie into Carter's arms as he takes a drink in his hand.

"From the time I was drafted, you've been the only coach I've ever had. Not only have you stepped up for me, but you've stepped up in ways every single one of the men here will carry with them for the rest of their lives."

Lexi squeezes my hand as my eyes start to fill with tears.

"What you've done for us goes beyond the game of football. I know I wouldn't be where I am today if it weren't for you." Alex clears his throat as he wraps an arm around Carter.

I smile back at him. "I'm glad—otherwise I wouldn't have my grandbabies."

Angie wiggles out of her papa's arms and runs over to me. "I love you, Grandpa."

"I love you too, munchkin."

"I know I wouldn't be here right now either, Coach," Jackson chimes in. "You made me pull my head out of my ass to see what I always had."

"I guess I should say thank you for that too," Tenley says. They both look exhausted. The faces of new parents.

"I'm glad you gave Rocky a job. Let's face it, she runs circles around all of us," Colin adds.

"You make it easy, Colin." Peyton laughs. "You stepped up for me, Coach, and I'll never forget it."

A stray tear falls loose.

Knox clears his throat. "I guess if we're saying our thanks, I owe you one too." Everyone laughs around him. "I was just a dumb kid when I came into this league. I didn't know my ass from my elbow, and you taught me more about life than anyone I know. Thanks, Coach."

"And thank you for teaching not only me, but every one of us here. Your mark will forever be left on the game of football," Frankie states.

I shake my head, trying to get my emotions under control. "Thank you all. You have no idea what that means to me."

"Seems like they like you," Lexi whispers, and I smile down at her. As hard as this decision is, it's also one of the easiest I've made. Because of this woman right here.

"We love you, Coach. And just because you're leaving, doesn't mean you won't forever be a Mountain Lion." Alex walks over to me, wrapping an arm around my shoulder. "To Coach Brooks!"

"Coach Brooks!" everyone echoes.

"Whaddya say, boys?" Colin shouts. "Think we can win another Super Bowl?"

"Hell yeah!" Knox replies. "To the Mountain Lions!"

"To the Mountain Lions!"

THE END

Want to see what the Mountain Lions are up to for the holidays? Read on for a bonus scene!

But wait! What about Logan?! Don't we get his story! Logan Winchester is going to be spinning off my BRAND NEW series...Dixon Creek Ranch! And while his story is coming, you can drop in on the Winchester Family. Scan the QR code below to grab a free short story now!

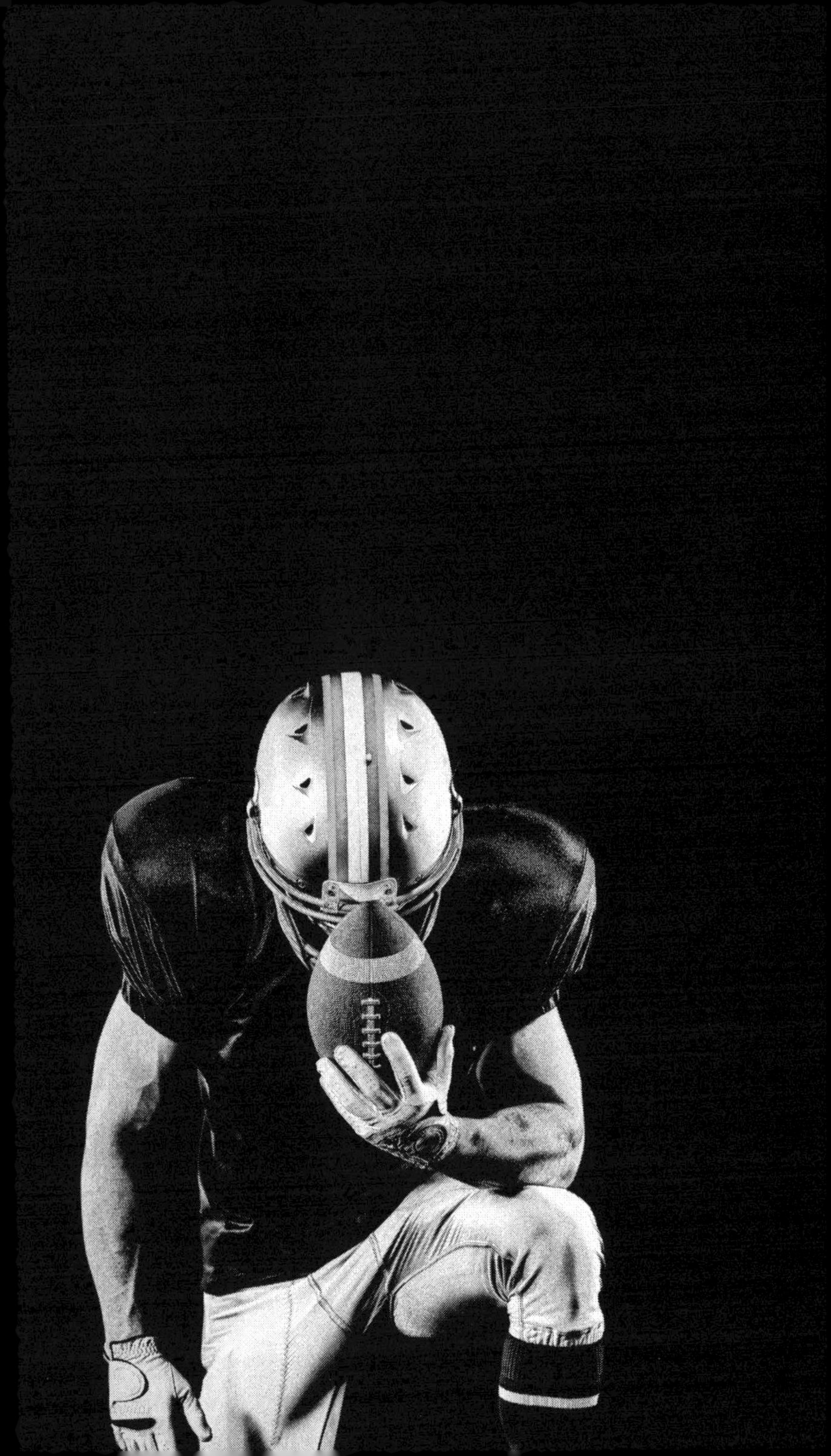

Bonus Scene

KNOX

This takes place between Illegal Contact and The Big Game.

"Are you sure I look okay?" Frankie smooths her hands over her sweater. It's a green sweater, with a giant gold bow sitting right on her chest.

"Is this something I can unwrap later?" I finger the gold material. For a December night, it's not as cold as it usually is.

Frankie laughs. "It doesn't quite work like that."

"Doesn't mean I won't be taking it off of you later." Wrapping her in my arms, I nip at her neck. Even after all these years, I still can't get enough of this woman.

"Knox, stop. I don't want a hickey before the team's holiday party."

"Now that's a damn shame." I follow Frankie through the parking lot of the team facility. "Who do you think is going to win the sweater contest?"

Frankie groans, leaning against the side of my truck.

"Did you really have to make a sweater with Colin's face all over it?"

"This is fucking awesome."

"I think you're going to be the only person to think that, Knox."

"Everyone is going to love it."

"I can't with you sometimes." She's shaking her head at me, but a smile graces those gorgeous lips of hers.

"You know you love me."

Frankie steps closer, pressing a kiss into the corner of my mouth. "I guess so."

"Wow, that's true love."

Linking hands with her, we walk into the team facility. Peyton and Colin are just ahead of us.

"Oh no," Peyton says, shaking her head as she sees me. It's then I see the sweater Colin is wearing. One with my face all over it.

"You took my idea!" We yell at each other at the same time.

"It's supposed to be an ugly sweater, Colin."

"I know. This is as ugly as it gets." He has a smile on his face that only Colin can wear.

"You mean as sexy as it gets." I grab his shoulder as we head inside the building.

"I'm definitely going to win the contest." Colin tries to wrap me in a headlock, but I shove him off.

"Are these two always like this?" I hear Frankie ask Peyton.

"Yes. We need a cocktail to deal with them." Peyton loops her arm through Frankie's and steers her toward the bar.

The entire practice area is decked out for the holidays. Lights are strung up from the beams. With the low lights, it looks like it could be snow. Trees are various sizes have

The Big Game

presents packed beneath them. A menorah lights up the wall next to it. Garlands are strung everywhere.

It's like the holidays exploded in here.

Colin and I meet them at the bar.

"I don't know if there is enough alcohol to deal with them," Frankie says, accepting a beer from Peyton.

"I take offense to that," I tell them, reaching around to grab my own drink.

"Yeah. We're delightful," Colin agrees.

"Are you though?" Alex appears behind us, Carter at his side.

"Don't you start too," I tell him.

"What are these sweaters?" Carter asks, eyeing both mine and Colin's.

"They are works of art," I tell him.

"You sure about that?" he questions me.

"Oh, like yours are better?" Colin waves a finger between the two of them.

"These are amazing." Alex waves his hand over his and Carter's matching Backstreet Boys ugly sweaters.

"Whatever you say, Young." I shake my head at him, sipping on my bourbon. "Whatever you say."

"I'm pretty sure I'm going to win." Jackson walks up, Tenley on his arm. "Mine is the best."

Whatever he's wearing looks like something Noah made. It says *Christmas with Daddy is the best* with handprints all over it. Clearly everyone is in the holiday spirit tonight.

"Well, no one can insult that," Colin grumbles.

"Exactly why I'm going to win." Jackson gives him a smug grin. "Tenley had it made for me."

"Where'd you get that made?" Carter asks her, looking a little more closely at the sweater.

"I'll send you a link." She winks back at him.

Parents.

"I know what Alex is getting for Christmas," Colin laughs.

"You'd love this if it was from Waffles."

"Fuck yeah, I would. His little paw prints all over it?" He starts thinking. "Actually, Tenley, would you send me the link too?"

"Sure thing." She's beaming back at him. I don't think I've ever seen her not smiling. Maybe if we lose a particularly hard game, but even then, she's always finding the upside.

"What are we going to make for Knox then?" Logan enters the fray.

"No Audrey this year?" I ask him, waving down the bartender for a drink.

"Nah." Something flashes across his face, but it's gone before I can pin it down. "Just me this year."

"Well it's great seeing you," Tenley says, pulling him in for a hug. "That touchdown on Sunday was brilliant."

That lights him up. "It felt really good."

"Way you dodged that defender? Taught you well."

"Way to be humble, Knox." Logan elbows me in the side.

"I know." I ruffle his hair.

"Get off me." He shoves me away.

"Where's your ugly sweater?" Jackson asks him.

"This is it."

"Wearing a Mountain Lions sweater? Not very creative." Colin shakes his head at him.

"Means I'll win."

"Who's picking the winner?" Jackson asks.

"That would be me, gentlemen."

Coach Brooks comes up behind us.

"Do we get bonus points for wearing Mountain Lions?"

"Suck up," Colin says under a cough.

"If anyone should get bonus points, it's me." Alex sips on his drink as we all stare at him.

"And why's that?" I ask.

"We gave Coach grandkids."

"Hey! You can't use that!" Colin barks out. "That's not fair. We're not related."

"Sucks to be you then," Alex laughs.

"I gave everyone Waffles. That should count for something."

"How long are you going to milk that?" Frankie asks.

"Et tu, Frankie?" Colin looks gutted.

"That's my girl." I wink at Frankie.

"That hurts, Knoxy."

"I'll be sure to judge fairly." Coach grabs his drink and turns away. "Be sure to behave tonight, boys."

"We will." We all answer on instinct.

"Wow. I need to know how he does that." Frankie looks at all of us. "He's got you trained."

"That's because we don't want to let him down," I tell her, moving to her side and wrapping an arm around her. I lean closer to her, my lips right at her ear. "Why do you think I always listened when you gave instructions?"

Frankie barks out a laugh. "That's what you call listening these last few years?"

"Hey!" My voice is more offended than I mean it to sound. There's no way I could ever be mad at Frankie.

"You know," Colin walks up to us, pushing me out of the way, "I think I can forgive you for that earlier comment. Anyone who gives Knox shit like Darlene will always be number one in my book."

A server comes by with a tray of appetizers. Everyone grabs a small plate and loads up.

"Is your only mission in life now to act like my grandmother?" I say, shoving a crab puff into my mouth.

Frankie is still laughing as Colin replies, "someone has to."

"I'm sure she'd be glad to know that you're keeping me in check."

I know without a doubt she would be. That's just how Grandma was--giving me shit one minute, then loving on me the next.

Cheerful music is loud over the speakers as food and drinks are consumed. Everyone is feeling festive tonight. Practice is light this week with the holidays coming up this weekend. Guys come and go over the course of the night, but us captains stick together. It's not often we get together with our partners, but it makes the night that much better. Being able to share it with the people we love most.

I don't know how much time has passed before Coach Brooks is at the mic.

"Alright everyone. Can I please have your attention?" His voice echoes through the speakers in the room. It quiets immediately.

"I want to thank all of you, especially the families tonight. Doing what we do isn't easy, and we couldn't do it without your love and support, so thank you."

I tug Frankie a little closer to me. I know exactly what Coach is talking about. The guys all have their partners that they go home to. But it's special that Frankie and I get to go home together.

She knows me in a way no one else ever will. We can be talking football one minute and then lose ourselves in each other the next. I wouldn't have it any other way.

Football and Frankie. That's all I'll ever need.

"Now, I know all of you are waiting to find out the winner of the ugly sweater contest."

All the guys stand a bit straighter next to me.

"Winchester."

"Are you shitting me?" Colin bellows, looking around the room. "Mine is clearly the ugliest."

"You mean sexiest," I argue again.

"This was rigged."

"Sorry, James. Can't beat perfection." Logan slaps him on the shoulder as he walks up to get what looks like a child's soccer trophy. His light-up Mountain Lions sweater is pretty great.

"I'll be sure to cheer you up." Peyton pecks him on the cheek. That stops him in his tracks.

"Well gentlemen, I think I'm calling it a night." Colin grabs Peyton and pulls her along behind him.

"God, could you be any more obvious?" She tells him as they walk out the door.

"I think we might call it a night, too." Alex yawns. "Need to relieve the babysitter."

"We should too," Tenley agrees.

"See you guys at practice." Jackson gives us each a back slap before wrapping an arm around Tenley and leaving.

"Knox. Frankie." Alex nods at both of us before him and Carter follow suit.

Logan is nowhere to be found.

Leaving just me and Frankie. The room is emptying out around us, now that the main event has happened.

"What do you say, Knox? Want to head home?" Frankie wraps both her arms around me.

I dip my head down a fraction of an inch, finding the shell of her ear. "Do I finally get to unwrap you from this sweater?"

Her fingers dig into my side, letting me know how much she likes the idea.

"Are you sure you're ready to see what's underneath?"

Pulling back, there's heat in Frankie's eyes.

"There's more than just this?"

Fuck me. Even after all these years, Frankie still drives me crazy with need. I'll never stop wanting this woman.

"If you think this is the best part," she waves a hand over the sweater, "then you are sorely mistaken."

"Fuck. We need to go. Now."

Frankie spins on her heel, walking out of the building. My vision tunnels to the sway of her ass. It was a great night with the guys. But tonight, with Frankie?

I'll be unwrapping the best present ever.

Author's Note

Book 12 is out in the world!

THE DENVER MOUNTAIN LIONS ARE FINALLY WORLD CHAMPS!!

I seriously can't believe how many of you messaged me that they hadn't won yet…all in due time ;) I cried as I wrote this story because I knew it was the end. I really can't believe the Mountain Lions series is over. This group of guys—this family—means so much to me, that I'm tearing up as I write this. As a lover of the Indianapolis Colts (even still as they are working really hard for that top draft pick this year), I knew I wanted to write a football romance. I have so much love for this team that I don't know if I'll ever really leave them behind. At least for now I won't be, because Logan's story is coming next year!!

There's so many wonderful people I want to thank. All my author and book friends…when I made the move full time to author me this year, so many of you jumped to support me and I can't thank you enough for your support! You know who you are and you are incredible <3

To my street team…some of you have been with me since the very beginning and I don't know what I did to deserve your support! Your excitement for my books always puts a smile on my face!

To my reader group, The Travelers…I love getting to hang out with you all!

To all the readers, bookstagrammers, booktokers and bloggers who read my books and share the love…I wouldn't be anywhere without you!

<3 Emily

About the Author

After winning a Young Author's Award in second grade, Emily Silver was destined to be a writer. She loves writing strong heroines and the swoony men who fall for them.

A lover of all things romance, Emily started writing books set in her favorite places around the world. As an avid traveler, she's been to all seven continents and sailed around the globe.

When she's not writing, Emily can be found sipping cocktails on her porch, reading all the romance she can get her hands on and planning her next big adventure!

Find her on social media to stay up to date on all her adventures and upcoming releases!

Also by Emily Silver

The Denver Mountain Lions

Roughing The Kicker

Pass Interference

Sideline Infraction

Illegal Contact

The Big Game

Dixon Creek Ranch

Yours To Lose - newsletter bonus story

Yours to Take - coming March 23, 2023

Yours to Hold - coming June 29, 2023

Yours to Be - coming August 24, 2023

Yours to Forget - coming November 16, 2023

Off the Deep End — A standalone, MM sports romance

The Ainsworth Royals

Royal Reckoning

Reckless Royal

Royal Relations

Royal Roots

Royal Ties

The Love Abroad Series

An Icy Infatuation

A French Fling

A Sydney Surprise

Get all my titles now:

Made in the USA
Columbia, SC
21 July 2023